IF
GRACE IS
DEAD,
I KILLED HER

T.G. STARR

If Grace is Dead, I Killed Her

First published in Australia in 2021
Copyright © 2021 Westminster Designs Pty Ltd

ISBN 978-1-925422-40-5

This book is a work of fiction. Names, characters, places, and incidents are either the author's imagination or are used fictitiously. Any resemblance to actual persons, living or dead, events or locales is entirely coincidental.

Amazing Grace Lyrics by John Newton Music by Edwin O Excell

Book cover design by Kirstie Minifie

www.tgstarr.com

DEDICATION

The Golden book series is dedicated to the Graces who have been bullied and felt pushed to the edge.

May this story help you dig down deep and find the strength to rise above.

And to the Maddies in the world, may you embrace the opportunity to change the story before the damage is done.

Most importantly, this book is dedicated to YOU. No matter who you are, whether a Grace, a Maddie, or someone in between.

May you find the courage to stand up for both yourself and others.

Together, we can make it Stop!

We can put an end to bullying ... once and for all.

ONE

If Grace is dead, I killed her.

With every passing moment, it was becoming more apparent that Grace probably *was* dead. If she were, there would be no question as to who had killed her. Maddie had. She knew it. Her friends knew it. And now her family, Grace's parents, and the sheriff knew it too.

Maddie couldn't shake the reality as she sat on her bed. Clutching her long slender legs, she nervously rocked back and forth.

If she is dead, my life will be over! She thought, not even aware of the irony. Grace Harwood was missing. An impending sense of doom engulfed Maddie. *No teenager, not even Grace, would run away and not take their phone.*

How would she keep in touch?

Maddie was growing more certain something terrible had happened. If only she hadn't pushed Grace over the edge.

How had it all gotten so far out of control?

What have I done?

TWO

A few months earlier.

Maddie chatted on the phone with her best friend, Echo Blaze. "What are you wearing tomorrow? Got a fit picked?" Echo asked.

"I dunno, I haven't thought much about it," Maddie lied. The truth of the matter was that she had spent a good chunk of the summer thinking about it. You only get one chance to make a good impression on your first day of high school. She had meticulously crafted her image for the new school year, and of course, her wardrobe was a crucial part of the plan.

Living in a single-mother household, the family budget didn't leave much room for new clothes. Maddie's mother, Elodie, worked at Striplings - the best (and only) department store in Pine Cove. The monthly paycheck barely covered the bills and Mom's vodka tab. Still, the job came with an employee discount, which gave her Grandma Betty some relief as she was the one who bought Maddie's clothes. Maddie appreciated her grandma, always doing whatever she could to make things better, but hated costing her so much money. So, on occasion, Maddie would drop by the store and "forget" to pay for outfits. Between Grandma Betty's generosity and her own five-finger discount, as she liked to call it, she had racked up a small but striking selection of clothes.

Before her big sister, Ashley moved out, space was limited in the small bedroom. Now the unused twin bed provided the ideal area to lay out the entire contents of her closet.

"I think we should wear red," Echo said. Maddie laughed. "I wear red all the time."

"I mean all of us," Echo clarified. "Don't tell me just because we're in high school you're going to bail out on tradition."

"I haven't decided on that ... but I'm wearing whatever I wear." Maddie glanced over her outfit choices. "We can wear red on Fridays. How's that?"

Echo sighed. "Well, whatever we wear, we're gonna *own* Pine Cove High just like we owned Pine Cove Middle School, ya know? And yes, to wear red on Fridays. I'll let everyone know. We're gonna own the school by Friday, so we'll celebrate in red."

*

The following morning Maddie dressed quickly, smiling at her reflection in the full-sized mirror mounted on the back of her bedroom door. Beneath her short denim shorts, her long and slender legs were the envy of many girls at school. Some girls spent hours baking in the sun to tan theirs, but Maddie was never into the torture. She rather liked her pale complexion, and since *she* set the standards in her group, that was what counted. She completed the outfit with a candy-apple-red crop top and strappy sandals.

A few more curves would be nice. Maddie hoped they'd come soon. She applied a layer of mascara to bring out her crystal blue eyes, wishing they were just a little bluer. *But these shorts should do the trick.* She wondered if she'd get in trouble for her short shorts on her first day of school. In a way, she really didn't care if it got her noticed, and she was pretty sure it would. Deep inside, Maddie didn't just *want* to get noticed. She *needed* to get noticed. It was a fact she hid from herself as much as she hid it from others - most of the time.

She needed to feel as though she was important, even just for a moment, and it didn't matter who made her feel that way. Her mother sure didn't act as though Maddie was important. She was too focused on herself.

Back in elementary school, she'd hated being the tallest girl in the class and how some kids made fun of her, calling her the "Mad Giraffe." The comments hurt her feelings back then, but now she was hell-bent on proving to everyone that she didn't care. Sometimes, she even had herself fooled.

She ran a brush through her dark brown hair and

noticed it was longer than her shorts were. Her once-awkward long legs and slender figure got her plenty of attention these days: comments and stares from the boys and envy from the girls. She'd spent all of middle school building an empire. She had a following, and she was in control – on the outside at least.

*

Maddie was in high spirits as she left the house. Today was going to be a new start – high school. Maddie loved the thrill of a fresh start. She strolled down the sidewalk to meet Echo before school. They always met at the park. It was the only park in the small postcard-perfect mountain town of Pine Cove, Colorado. The two girls first met there when they were in preschool – their mothers took them for playdates. Echo had always been a cute and funny girl, with a crooked smile that lit up her face. Even at a young age, Maddie knew Echo looked up to her – maybe a little too much. Maddie had never been sure why. Perhaps she thought of Maddie as a big sister and felt the same way about her as Maddie felt about Ashley. Or, maybe she found it more comfortable to be in Maddie's shadow. But would Echo still feel the same way about her if she knew her insecurities and all? Maddie wasn't taking any chances.

Echo didn't know Maddie was envious of her – not because of her looks or personality but because of her family life. Her parents were loving, kind and as a family, they had lots of fun. Although a little too protective at times, her older brother, Elmo, was a very caring person ... and cute. If he weren't like a brother to her and too old, Maddie would have easily had a crush on him.

Maddie knew the Blaze family thought the world of her. Their house was her home away from home. She was even included in the camping trips and summer vacations. Still, it wasn't the same.

"That outfit is fire!" Echo was perched on the swing.

Maddie gave a nod.

When Maddie started the Scarlet Squad in middle school, Echo was her first recruit. She was sure she could count on her best friend, and Echo had not let her down. They were hot, they were mean, and no one could touch them.

The two took off along a cobblestone pathway through the mountainside park to the sidewalk that led to the school.

"Nervous?" Echo struggled to keep up with Maddie's long legs on the steep rocky incline.

"Are you kidding me?" Maddie rolled her eyes and shook her head. "Why would *I* be nervous?" The truth was that she was terrified. But that was her little secret. If she could keep everyone walking on eggshells, she knew she would ace the day and the entire year. Being mean had its advantages.

"OMG, you're hard to keep up with," Echo trailed behind. "No kidding!"

"In more ways than one."

The girls rounded a curve in the path. "Whoa!" a voice called out as a guy almost walked right into them.

"Whoa is right!" Echo exclaimed, stopping for a minute to admire the green-eyed guy with brown hippie-looking hair.

"Seriously?" Maddie snapped, continuing her mission to get to school. She had no intentions of letting on to the fact that she thought he was hot.

The green-eyed guy caught up to Maddie as Echo followed behind. First day of high school?" he asked, slowing down to let Echo catch up.

Crap ... is it that obvious? Maddie picked up her pace. "Yup, and I don't wanna be late."

Never let boys feel superior ... or anyone, for that matter.

"Have a good one," the guy said as they reached the parking lot and parted ways. He took off toward the side entrance. The girls walked on to the main door.

Maddie found it interesting that he didn't flirt with her, nor did he seem intimidated by her. Most guys acted one way or the other. She'd have to keep an eye on this one.

*

As expected, Maddie was summoned to the principal's office and told never to wear her short shorts again. She silently thanked the principal for boosting her rebel image in front of everyone on the first day. Not much else of interest happened until the walk home when the girls ran into Green Eyes again.

"School go OK?" he asked.

"Except for Freeman going off on Mad," Echo giggled.

"And ... you must be ... Mad?" he asked. "I don't mean *mad*, mad ... but, your name is ... Mad?" The girls cracked up, but the green-eyed guy was fully confident and composed. Most people they laughed at got embarrassed.

"Maddison ... Maddie ... Hunter." Maddie wondered why she had given her full name. *Why not give him your phone number, too?*

"And I'm Echo."

"Jake Taylor," he replied. "Well, this is the way I go home. Nice to meet you, ladies." He turned left, down the road out of town, while the girls turned off right towards the park.

"Sophia and Kaitlyn said they have every class together," Echo said. "How'd they manage that? You'd think they were joined at the hips ..."

Maddie didn't say a word.

"Uh ... you *don't* think Mrs. Motts is a witch?" Echo asked. "Sad that the one class we have together is with her ... and is math ... I *hate* math ... I hate the kids in the class too ... well, except you ... and me ..."

"Huh?"

Echo laughed and ran to her favorite swing. "Are

you ignoring me, Mad? Maddie ... *Maddison Hunter?*"

Maddie knew Echo was making fun of her but let it slide. She was surprised herself, so how could she blame Echo? Green-Eyes Jake had made a definite impression on her, and she was finding it hard to shake it off.

THREE

Maddie and Echo wore red to the first school dance. They'd been walking to school with Jake for weeks before Maddie finally asked if he was going to the dance. He'd been nonchalant, saying it wasn't his thing. But Maddie spotted him across the school gym straight away. Butterflies somersaulted in her stomach. He wasn't her type at all – typically, she would have had a crush on a class stud, the football team's quarterback, or a basketball star. Not a quiet guy like Jake. But he had a way about him that she found intriguing. Her heart skipped a beat. She could hardly believe he was there.

All of Maddie's friendship group, the Scarlet Squad, were at the dance. Sophia and Kaitlyn wore matching red sweaters.

Can't they ever do something original? Why do they always have to dress alike?

Arkadia had brought along her "on-again, off-again" boyfriend, Chad, and some newbie she introduced as SJ. Chad's brother, Kyle, was hanging with them too.

Kyle is so basic. Why did she bring him along?

As Jake walked through the busy gym towards her, Maddie felt like a spotlight was lighting him up. He took her hand and led her to the dance floor. She was walking on air – it felt like a scene out of a movie. Her heart beat hard. She wanted to look cool but couldn't help grinning. The guy could dance – he had moves that swept Maddie off her feet. She hoped everyone was watching.

After a couple of songs, she promised Jake she'd be back in a moment. She returned to her group and grabbed Echo's hand, pulling her towards the restroom.

"Don't you dare hook up with Kyle the Pile," Maddie warned, having seen Echo chatting to him.

"Speaking of hooking up ..." Echo stopped short when Maddie shot her an evil eye.

"Speaking of *shutting* up."

"Anyway, let's fix that new girl SJ up with Pile o' Poop. You know she's got to go through the squad initiation if she's gonna hang with us."

Maddie was never fond of the idea of anyone joining their tight group. She didn't like that Arkadia had brought along her boyfriend Chad without clearing it but bringing Kyle, as well as some straight-looking new girl, had crossed the line. The new girl would pay the price, and the price would be humiliation.

"Tell her she has a secret admirer who wants to go out with her and tell him the same," Maddie ordered as they walked back to the gym.

The band began to play again, and Maddie disappeared with Jake onto the dance floor. They danced nonstop until it was over at 10 pm.

I knew high school was going to be lit. See all the stares and jealous looks from the other girls?

Jake walked Maddie to the turn-off. Echo followed behind, chattering to Maddie about how happy Kyle was that he had an admirer. And how funny it was that SJ was stupid enough to think she had one too.

"I think I'm going to like it here in Pine Cove," Jake told Maddie.

"Why did you move here?" She couldn't imagine anyone voluntarily moving to such a sleepy town.

"My grandfather is growing old and wanted to move here, so we made it happen."

"We're from Indiana, and I guess he had lived there his whole life and wanted a change. He'd driven through here years ago, touring the Rockies with Grandma. He swore he'd move here one day, and now he has. My parents sold their farm and are starting a hemp farm over by Miramonte Lake. You should come by and check it out some time."

Maddie grinned.

Jake took Maddie gently in his arms and kissed her. "Good night," he said, his green eyes piercing hers.

Maddie tried to speak, but no words came. Finally, she managed to whisper, "Good night, Jake."

FOUR

It was Friday, November 10, Maddie's birthday. She was finally fourteen. She and Jake had been an item since the dance, and all the other girls were envious.

Jake had turned sixteen in October and passed his driving test straight away. He bought a Mustang with the money he had saved from working all summer for his grandfather. It was an older model, but Maddie thought it suited him well. It was a little on the rugged side, like him. Best of all, it was fire-engine red, her favorite color. She suspected he had chosen red on purpose, and, even if he didn't, it was nice to think he did. Plus, none of the other freshman girls had a boyfriend with a car!

She hadn't mentioned Jake to her mom, obviously. Her mom was weird about boys. She'd never let her go out with a junior, especially a junior with a car. Probably because, according to her, Maddie's dad couldn't keep his pants zipped up. He'd left when Maddie was four. Maddie wondered if her dad would have been protective over his teenage daughters, like Echo's dad and brother were. How would he have reacted if he knew seventeen-year-old Ashley lived with her boyfriend and was eight months pregnant?

The cold wind was blowing as Maddie walked to the park to meet Echo. "I have a little something for you," Echo had told her on the phone. "But you've got to come to the park to get it."

Maddie wrapped her coat around her, wishing she hadn't worn such a short skirt. She spotted Echo and picked up her pace, curious to see what her bestie had gotten her.

Out of nowhere, Jake pulled up in his Mustang and shouted, "Jump in!"

"How'd you know I was here?" Maddie asked. "Are you stalking me?"

She reached over and gave him a peck on the cheek, then turned the heater and the stereo up full blast. Echo climbed in the back and gave Jake a thumbs up. He peeled out and sped off. "Why wouldn't I be?" Jake laughed. "A 'good looking' girl like you ..."

Maddie expected Echo to give her the present she had mentioned. But she didn't. No one wished her a happy birthday either. Aside from the blaring music, everyone was eerily silent. "You two are being awfully shady."

Neither Jake nor Echo said a word. Maddie turned the stereo down and asked, "All right ... why is everyone so weird?"

She got no reply. Within a few minutes, they were at Lake Miramonte at the edge of town. Jake pulled into the parking lot next to the Ice Hut skating rink.

Maddie wrinkled her brow. "Oh ... kay ..." she said slightly louder than a whisper. She had been hoping Jake was taking her out somewhere nice for her birthday, just the two of them, but that obviously wasn't happening.

Jake parked the car, and Echo jumped out. "Later!" she cried as she darted through the parking lot to the Ice Hut.

Maddie didn't budge.

"What's wrong? Don't you like to ice skate?" Jake had a mischievous smile, his green eyes glowing.

Maddie shrugged her shoulders. "I used to ... when I was a kid. Haven't been in years, though."

Since the time in third grade, when I fell over on the ice, everyone laughed at me. "Serious? I'd take you for an ice-skating queen with those knock-out long legs." Maddie glowed inside. Maybe this wouldn't be so bad.

Jake got out of the car and walked over to the passenger door. "Come on," he coaxed. "I'll buy you a hot cocoa for your birthday."

"With tiny marshmallows in it?" she smiled. "Yup ... with tiny marshmallows in it."

Maddie hopped out, and the two rushed through the cold rain that was beginning to fall. They hurried inside the Hut to warm up. Just as Maddie stepped in, everyone jumped out at her. "Happy Birthday!"

Jake placed a beautiful red rose in her hands. She felt like a princess. She hoped someone was taking a photo so she could post it later.

Everyone from her circle was there: Echo, Sophia, Kaitlyn, and Arkadia, with Chad. His brother Kyle the Pile had even tagged along.

People outside her circle were there too: Chloe, Isabella, and Jasmine from the popular girl group. Maddie couldn't believe they came to her party. They were always friendly and smiley to her face, but Maddie knew they didn't think she was good enough, pretty enough, or tight enough to hang out with them. Besides, they were the very three girls who had laughed when she fell on the ice. She would never forget that day.

Plain Face Grace and No Action Jackson were there in the shadows. Grace wasn't plain. She was super smart but shy and reserved. Maddie despised her and made the name up to humiliate her. It worked. Jackson was the local minister's equally boring son. Maddie had known them both since elementary school. They were two goody-goodies who even brought their Bibles to school to read once they finished their work in study hall. Being nerds, Maddie had never paid them much attention until one day in sixth grade. The school year was ending, and a father-daughter event was planned. "Maddie, I know you don't have a father," Grace said. "There is a wonderful man in my church who would be happy to take you. You would love him. He's so sweet and ...."

Maddie had been furious. How dare Grace call her out like that? She wasn't some charity project. Just because she didn't have a father living with her didn't make her some kind of a misfit orphan.

Grace had stood speechless as Maddie snapped. "I *have* a father."

The look on Maddie's face warned Jackson not to intervene, but he did. "Hey, you OK, Grace?"

"I was just telling Maddie about Brother Joseph."

"He's a really great Christian guy," Jackson had told Maddie. "He has a real heart of—" Jackson stopped midsentence as Maddie's fury gained pace. With a hefty shove, Maddie pushed Jackson into the lockers.

"I don't need some stupid man from your church to take me to some lame school thing," she'd fumed. "I *do* have a father. He's just not here. He's in California making a ton of money. He's rich and way better than your dad ... the preacher man ... what a loser!"

Maddie and Grace's history went back even further, though. When Maddie's father left, Grace's parents had reached out to her mother. They welcomed them into their church. Maddie and Grace attended Sunday school together and vacation Bible school for one week every summer.

Maddie was too young to figure it out, but when they started second grade, it became apparent the other kids thought Grace was a nerd. "Why do you hang out with her?" Isabella had asked. "She's such a square."

Maddie didn't even know what a "square" was, but she did know it wasn't good and that if she wanted to be liked by Isabella and her pretty friends, Chloe and Jasmine, she would have to stop playing with Grace. By that time, Elodie's drinking was getting way out of hand. Maddie started to feel embarrassed how Mom showed up to church hungover and always caused a scene.

One Sunday lunch, when Elodie tried to kiss Grace's uncle in front of everyone, Grace's father drew the line. "I believe you should do one of two things," he told her. "Either get help for your alcohol problem or keep your distance."

Grace's dad had offered to get Mom into rehab, and at first, she agreed to it. Maddie was excited that she and Ashley were going to stay with the Harwood family. But then everything fell apart. Mom said it was all just a big set-up. Maddie never was quite sure what *really* happened. Somewhere along the way, she lost faith in the Harwoods, her mother, and in God.

Maddie hated how Grace tried to stick her nose in to help. She didn't want Grace or anyone else to pity her. When the stunt in the sixth grade happened, she rallied up the Scarlet Squad and made it clear that Grace was on her wrong side and would now be known as Plain Face Grace. And Jackson too. They were both fair game for Scarlet Squad retaliation from that day forward.

How did they get invited anyway? Jake, you suck at guest lists.

"Hope you don't mind that I invited a few friends to join us," Jake whispered. He ran to the snack bar and returned with a mug of cocoa overflowing with marshmallows.

Maddie didn't like half the people who were there. But the fact that Jake had planned a surprise party for her made up for his shortcomings. She knew full well that he was not a social person.

Aside from Maddie and sometimes Echo, he was a loner. So, she appreciated the gesture and decided to make the best of it. After all, it was her birthday, and she was finally fourteen.

Jake took Maddie over to pick out skates. "The party is lit, Jake," Maddie sipped on her cocoa. "Thank you."

Jake smiled and winked a green eye." Every princess should have a party. Especially *my* princess."

Maddie was hyper-aware that Chloe, Isabella, and Jasmine were standing right next to her, picking through the skates too. She hoped they'd heard the princess bit.

"You said size eight?" he asked, holding up a pair of pink skates. "Here's some." Maddie scowled. "Oh my god, Jake. Pink. You'll never catch me in pink *anything.*"

"Good thing I didn't get you a pink rose."

"For sure," Maddie replied. Then she noticed Chloe was wearing a pink sweater. Her long blonde hair was in a pink scrunchy, and her oversized earrings were pink as well. Oops.

"Happy birthday, *Maggie*." Maddie couldn't tell if Chloe was silly or sarcastic. "Maddie," Jake told her.

"Oh ... that's right ... Maddie," she corrected herself with a quick side glance over to Isabella and Jasmine. "Thanks for the heads up, Jake," Chloe shot him a flirty flash that Maddie didn't miss.

Jake was oblivious to what was going on. "Well, guess I'm flattered you got my name right."

Maddie's cocoa suddenly tasted sickly sweet, and the rose she'd carried proudly now seemed sad and wilted. She forced herself to stand up straight, throw her shoulders back and take hold of Jake's hand as the three popular girls walked off with their skates.

Chloe's name would need to come up in the next Scarlet Squad meeting. They'd find a way to get back at her.

Maddie laced up her skates. She didn't remember them being so challenging to walk on. Jake seemed confident, though, and helped her down the steps to the ice. "You don't seem like the type of guy who ice skates," she confided. "No offense."

Jake looked surprised. "Obviously, you don't come here very often. I've been ice skating since I was four. Can ya believe they have ice skating rinks in

Indiana? Nothin' much else to do there. So, when I moved here this summer and learned about the Hut, I started coming here."

Chloe, Isabella, and Jasmine were gracefully gliding around the rink. Maddie wished she wasn't so shaky. She must look like a dumb little kid, or even worse, like the gangly giraffe of elementary school. The one that stacked in the middle of the rink in third grade busting her lip, limbs everywhere, the laughing-stock of the popular girls. An announcement came over the loudspeaker.

"Birthday girl on the ice!" a baritone voice called out. "Let's give a hand to Maddie, who is fabulous fourteen today."

There was a roar of applause. Maddie managed a big, fake smile. This is not how she wanted everyone to see her. She wanted to disappear into a hole.

Jake held out his hand, and the two skated to the music. Jake was so light on his feet, seamlessly helping her balance.

Echo came up full blast behind them. "I can't s-s-s-t-t-t-o-p!" she screamed, stumbling on her skates and sliding down the length of the ice rink until she finally came to a halt. Because Maddie had refused to go skating since elementary school, Echo had refused as well. Now they both sucked. Maddie couldn't help but giggle at Echo's crash.

"Shouldn't we go help her?" Jake was pulling Maddie towards Echo.

"Nah, she's fine. Leave her," Maddie insisted. She didn't want to risk falling over herself when trying to help Echo up. Not in this short skirt.

Jake gave her a bewildered look.

After Echo dusted off, she joined them. "Hey, Mad, check it out," she said, pointing to the entrance door. It was SJ, the new girl. "She's coming to meet her secret admirer."

"Oh, how funny." Maddie cracked up. "We've gotta see this."

The girls skated over to the snack bar, where SJ was carrying something in a large plastic bag. She ran a nervous hand through her hair as she looked from one side to the other in search of the secret admirer she was supposed to meet.

Echo poked Maddie, pointing to Kyle the Pile, who was also walking up to the snack bar.

SJ sat on a corner barstool, still looking around for her date as Kyle approached the snack bar and looked all around. Maddie couldn't hold back her laughter. She couldn't believe they were together and still looking for their secret dates. She wondered how long it would take them to catch on. "Are you stupid or something?" she exclaimed, accidentally a little louder than she meant to.

"That's just mean, Mad," a voice said from behind her. It was Jake.

Maddie's mouth fell open. "Uh, I thought you were skating," she said. "We're just getting a snack."

Jake wasn't buying it, and Maddie knew it. She eased over to the snack bar to order a candy bar.

"Oh, hi SJ!" Maddie pretended she hadn't been watching her for the past few minutes.

SJ rustled with the plastic sack beside her and pulled out a birthday cake. It was white with pink roses. "Happy Birthday Maddie," it read.

"How ... sweet!" Maddie giggled. "And how ... pink! Adorable." She went ahead and ordered a chocolate bar. There was no way she was eating a pink cake.

Echo pushed her way in between Maddie and SJ. "I'll have a piece," she told SJ, who pulled out a plastic knife, cut a piece of cake, and put it on a pink napkin.

"Well, aren't you the cat's pajamas?" Echo laughed. "Don't you think, Kyle?" She turned to Kyle.

Kyle nodded his head politely, still looking around the room for his secret admirer.

"By the way, Kyle, meet SJ, your blind date. And SJ, meet Kyle, your secret admirer." Echo looked at Maddie for an approving nod.

Kyle's eyes widened. SJ's jaw dropped. Maddie couldn't contain her laughter at how astonished they both looked. Kyle was an idiot. SJ had pimples and a crooked nose. They must realize no one would be their secret admirers in real life. She was sure they'd both be so embarrassed that they'd never be able to look at each other again. She pulled Echo's arm, and the girls stumbled back onto the ice, holding onto each other laughing until tears ran down both their faces.

"Where'd Jake go?" Echo asked when they stopped to catch their breath.

Maddie shrugged her shoulders. "I dunno ... I don't see him anywhere." She pulled out her phone and tried calling him, with no answer. She sent a text full of question marks.

Plain Face Grace was standing near them. "Happ—" she began, but Maddie cut her right off. "What made *you* think you should come to this party?"

Grace slowly skated off.

Skating was too hard without Jake to lean on. Maddie rechecked her phone. There was a bunch of missed calls from her mom. Ergh. Nothing from Jake. Maybe he had a family emergency or something. But how was she meant to get home without his car? Why did he think he could just leave her here looking like a loner at her own party?

"I'm done with this dump. Ready to get outta here?"

"Sure," Echo agreed. Maddie noticed Echo glance back at their friends on the skating rink as if she wanted to stay. Maddie knew she'd be loyal, though.

The girls skated off the ice and swapped their skates for shoes. By the time they got to the exit door, Maddie had noticed someone all too familiar was standing in the doorway. It was her mother.

"What do you think you're doing, young lady?" There stood Elodie in her way-too-bright and way-too-tight orange and yellow fuzzy sweater, with her big blonde hair box-dyed two shades too light. As usual, she was wearing her caked-on makeup.

Maddie wished she could sneak out the side door and take off running. Her mother had been drinking. She got very loud when she drank.

"Maddison Hunter ... you are grounded!"

A hush fell over the crowd. Maddie knew everyone would be watching. She walked to her mother, hoping she would lower her voice and they could just leave quietly. She had to minimize the amount of cred she was about to lose at school.

Elodie grabbed Maddie by the arm. "What ... you turn fourteen and think you don't have to ask if you can go somewhere now? How did you get here? Why did you think you could just sneak off?"

Maddie's face felt like it was on fire with embarrassment. She was sure everyone would be gossiping about this for weeks. She wondered how her mom had found her – but then again, it was a small town. She hoped her mom hadn't drunk-dialed too many people to find out.

Elodie dragged Maddie to the car. "I had a nice family party planned for you, Maddison ... everyone's waiting at home. I've been calling you. I can't believe you ruined it."

Maddie remembered her rose was back at the Ice

Hut. Her princess rose. Elodie started driving – there's no way she could get it back now.

*No, Mom ... you *ruined it! And now you're risking both of our lives driving home drunk. But what's new?*

FIVE

M addie texted Jake the whole way home in the car. She started feeling a bit worried about his lack of response. Maybe his battery was flat. Or he lost his phone at the rink or something. She couldn't even think ahead to school – her insides shrank with shame at how embarrassing her mom was.

She stepped into the house.

"Surprise!" her pregnant sister Ashley shouted as she popped up from behind the bar. "Happy Maddie Day!" her Grandma Betty appeared from the back hallway.

Ashley's boyfriend, Samuel, jumped out from his hiding spot in the walk-in pantry. "Happy BIG fourteen!"

Ew, why'd you have to bring him? Maddie had never liked Samuel. He gave her weird vibes. She was sure it was him she had seen walking out of the movie theater with someone other than her sister. It was a situation she had intended to investigate but had gotten so wrapped up in Jake, she'd forgotten.

Elodie poured herself a vodka tonic. "I told you they were all here waiting. If you don't answer your phone next time I call, I'll confiscate it."

Maddie clenched her jaw. She hated that her mom could take away freedoms just like that. "Anyway, happy birthday. It's hard to believe that just fourteen years ago, I was at Clarks getting some preggie snacks when my water broke. I thought I'd peed my pants, but ..."

"Mom, you are freaking me out," Ashley protested, protectively holding her baby bump as if it would fall out.

Elodie waved her eldest daughter off. "If you're old enough to do the crime ... you're old enough to do the time ... *and* to hear the war stories. Where was I? Oh, yeah ... so, Tom, the manager at the time, called the fire department, of all the stupid things. I wasn't on fire. I was having a baby."

"Mom!" Ashley snapped. "This isn't about you ... it's about Mad." Elodie pouted as she took a long swig of vodka.

"The drinking's going well then," Ashley said sarcastically. "Nice to see things have changed since I moved out."

Elodie slapped her hand on the table. "*That* is none of your business!"

Maddie sighed. She always hated when her sister and her mother argued, and they did whenever they were together. Ashley never hesitated to speak her mind, which Maddie wished she was better at where her mother was concerned. She had no problem telling people her age off. But when it came to her mom, she backed down, mostly because she feared the repercussions ... like getting grounded or having her phone confiscated.

A birthday cake appeared from the kitchen in Grandma's hands. Unlike the puke pink cake SJ had bought her, this one was nothing short of incredible – a chocolate cake made from scratch with chocolate ice cream on top. Grandma Betty was an excellent cook.

Maddie didn't want to be in a better mood. She was grounded, and she was stressed about Jake. But she couldn't hold back from enjoying the delicious cake and being around Ashley and Grandma Betty, who always made her feel better.

"How far along are you now, Ash?" Grandma Betty asked, reaching over to pat Ashley's bulging belly.

Ashley beamed. "Eight months today." Samuel leaned over and kissed her cheek. Maddie cringed.

"I just love you so much, Ash, and want the best for you. You made a granny out of me, you know ... my firstborn grandchild. I want the best for you, just like I wanted the best for your mom ... but she wouldn't listen either."

Elodie stood up, wobbled, and fell backward against the wall. "So, help me, God, that woman has been hell-bent on givin' me a hard time since you were conceived," she ranted to Ashley. "And I *was* married ... but nothin's good 'nuff for Grandma Betty."

"What's the point of bein' married if your husband's always cheatin' on ya? But you didn't listen... just kept bustin' out babies." Grandma retorted. Everyone knew this argument off by heart – it was wheeled out at most gatherings. There wasn't much heat in it anymore. "And one of them has a birthday today!" Ashley shouted.

"Maddie, I am so sorry the matriarchs of the family can't get along good enough to give you your one day."

"Well, doll, I can't stay long, so here's your present," Grandma Betty held out a blue box with an oversized white bow on it. "I hope it's the right size." She smiled and winked.

Maddie unwrapped the box and opened it. "W-w-w-h-h-a-t?" She was shocked to see a brand-new tablet. "Are you freakin' kidding me?" She flew into her grandma's arms.

"Thank you ... thank you ... thank you!"

Grandma laughed. "I guess it fits." She returned Maddie's hug and let herself out the side door. Then she stuck her head back inside the screen door, looked at Maddie, and said, "Lodie ... at least you did something right." She looked at Ashley. "Well, two things." She shut the door behind her and was gone.

Maddie couldn't wait to try out her new tablet. She'd only ever had her sister's hand-me-down phones that were at least two years behind by the time she got them. But as excited as she was, she really wanted to have a little chat time with her sister. She missed Ashley so much since she'd moved out. Ashley had never been a good influence. She was a wild child. But she'd been more of a mother to Maddie than Elodie ever had been. When Mom was busy drinking and going to the bars to chase men, it was Ashley who had taken care of her even though she had done so while sneaking cigarettes and mom's liquor stash.

"So ... am I havin' a grandson or a granddaughter?" Elodie slurred. "I don't know why you won't tell me. Cuz ... I never had a boy ... so we can have a boy ... girls are a pain."

Ashley ignored the question entirely. Samuel was already on the sofa, television remote in hand, and clicked on a football game.

"Maddison, I know about the junior," Mom continued, pointing a shaky finger at Maddie. "You're too young for a boyfriend. No boys until you're eighteen. I don't want you to see him again. There'll be hell to pay ... hear me?" She returned to her drink.

Maddie motioned for Ashley to meet her outside. The girls grabbed snuggle blankets to help them keep warm from the chilly night air. The porch was their favorite spot for sister talks, so their mother couldn't overhear them.

"Sup, sis?" Ashley asked as they sat side by side on the double swing.

"Mom." Maddie felt her throat tighten. "She

came to the Hut and dragged me out in front of everyone ... he had thrown me a surprise party."

"The junior?"

"Yes, the junior. Big deal, Ashley. Samuel's four years older than you are."

"And I'm pregnant! Don't follow what I'm doing." She paused. "Don't tell Mom, but we're having a boy. We're going to name him Liam James."

"Oh my god!" Maddie yelped. "Yay! I can't wait. I'm going to be his favorite aunt! I'll make sure of it!"

Ashley was cracking up. "Mad, Samuel doesn't have any siblings ... you'll be his *only* aunt."

"Then I'll for sure be his favorite!"

Ashley grew serious again. "I just want the best for you. Did Mom meet him? What's he like?"

"He's perfect, Ash," Maddie desperately tried to explain. "He's mad at me, though." Ashley frowned.

"For ...?"

"I dunno. Maybe for being mean ... you know, Scarlet Squad mean?"

Ashley shook her head. "Seriously, I don't know why you're such a *mean person* - you're a borderline bully. But I think I like this dude. Tell ya what, let me meet him, and I'll let you know ... I'm an excellent judge of character."

Samuel appeared at the glass door. "Ready, Mamma?"

Samuel had such a manipulative power over her sister, and it made Maddie sick.

Yeah ... excellent judge of character, sis.

*

Maddie managed to slip through the kitchen, grab her gift from Grandma Betty, and tiptoe up the stairs without waking her mother up from the kitchen table where she was crashed out. She quietly shut her bedroom door, threw herself onto her bed, and began checking out her new tablet.

Whoa ... TeenScene! She couldn't believe the app was ready to roll. She wasted no time signing up – it was easy. No birthday or any other credentials were required. The best thing was she could create as many accounts and usernames as she wanted. And so, the fun began.

The first profile she created was under the name of Kaylie. She copied and pasted a photo of a teenage girl she saw on an ad for an animal shelter in California. The girl was holding a snow-white Persian kitten. "That kitten will throw them off, don't you think, Shadow?" she asked her black cat. "Soft on the outside but evil underneath." Shadow rubbed her head against Maddie's cheek as if to agree.

She began to scour TeenScene to see if any of her friends or enemies had also joined. Nope, no Jake. She kept looking. She knew Echo wasn't even aware the app was out yet. Chloe was on but not active yet; she had no photo or information. But Grace was on there with her plain-faced photo and a cheery little motto: "Smile, and the world smiles back at you."

Oh, brother. No wonder I hate her.

Maddie sent Grace a friend request, under Kaylie's name, of course. Within seconds Grace accepted the request.

Talk about desperate.

Maddie sent her first message.

Kaylie: r u rele from Colorado?

Grace: Sure am. Born and raised here in a little town called Pine Cove.

Kaylie: lucky chick! i'm from cali

Grace: That's even cooler!

Kaylie: Btw, i like ur life motto; r many of ur friends on Teen yet?

Grace: Nah. Not really. I have five friends on here, but Jackson's my only real friend.

Kaylie: oh, kewl, is he ur bf?

Grace: No.

Kaylie: do u like anyone?

Grace: Yes. But no one knows.

Kaylie: awesome ... a secret crush

Grace: I guess so. Do you have a boyfriend?

Kaylie: tons of them

Maddie couldn't control her laughter. Two hours had flown by. She had even forgotten about Jake, well, almost. She coaxed Shadow back up on the bed, kissed her, and turned her bedside lamp off.

Sweet dreams, mean girl. Even if you can't skate for crap and your family's a train wreck, and you're the laughingstock of school and your boyfriend's missing in action … you are very good at being bad, you know.

SIX

It was Monday morning. Time to face everyone at school. Maddie dressed in her favorite red sweater and a pair of skin-tight jeans. She brushed her hair long over her shoulders and then checked herself in the full-size mirror, wishing she liked what she saw more than she did. *Maybe I should dye my hair another color? I wish I had bigger boobs.*

Jake still hadn't replied. She didn't know whether to be angry or scared.

Echo met her at the park. "That was messed up at your party."

Maddie shivered in the cold morning. Her sweater was cute but not warm enough for the wind today.

"I mean, I've seen your mom drunk and seen her crazy, but I've never seen her go off like that before. Are you OK?"

Maddie had ignored Echo's texts all weekend. She hadn't known how to respond to her. It was easier to act happy as a fake profile online. The two walked towards the school. Maddie was unusually quiet. "Yeah. I'm grounded for two weeks."

The sound of a familiar car came up behind them. "Get in!" a voice called out.

Maddie looked back. It was Jake with his head out the car window. So, he *was* OK. "You guys are going to freeze."

Maddie jumped in the front passenger seat, and Echo hopped in the back. "Thanks," Maddie said, shooting flirty eyes Jake's way.

Jake remained stoic. He didn't smile or flash his grassy green eyes in return. "I just didn't want you ladies to walk in the cold," he said without emotion.

The school was only minutes away. So, when Jake drove through the parking lot, Maddie knew she had better make a move while she had his attention.

"Why did you leave the Hut in the middle of my party? Did you get my calls and texts?"

Jake found a spot to pull into and parked the car, leaving the engine running for the heater. Echo wasted no time in getting out. "Later!"

"I guess ... I guess you took me by surprise, Mad," he struggled to explain. "I had never really seen you around people, except for the dance. I thought it was my imagination then. But at your party, you were ... well ... you weren't a very nice person to quite a few people."

Maddie wasn't sure whether to be hurt, angry, or ashamed.

"For one thing, I appreciate you throwing me the party ... but you didn't ask for a guest list," she said. "You don't even know those people, so why do you just assume it was *me* ... my fault?"

Jake looked her straight in the eyes. "It's the way you did it, Mad. I saw you laughing at those kids. And you didn't even want to help your best friend. I don't want to be with someone like that."

Maddie felt like she'd been punched in the stomach. Was he dumping her? She had a reputation to live up to. What would the others think? She let tears stream down her face. "I am so sorry. I didn't mean to be mean. I didn't mean any of it. I guess I'm just ... insecure. Yeah, I'm insecure and always have been because my father left. And my mom's a drunk. And my sister moved out and left me with her. If I were worth a crap, none of them would have left."

It was working. Jake was softening up. Maddie could feel it, and she couldn't have been more pleased. Then the warning school bell rang out.

"Oh no," Maddie grabbed her backpack. "Motts will come unglued if I'm late ... one point off our semester grade for every unexcused tardy."

Jake nodded. "I've got gym straight up, so I've gotta go play some basketball."

"See ya around?" Maddie questioned with playful pouty lips and puppy dog eyes to match.

Jake got his books, and they both got out of the car. Jake locked the doors. "Take care," he returned, with what Maddie hoped was a smile.

As Maddie was walking off, she glanced at her Boone and Durkes purse sitting on the floorboard of his car. *Genius. Simply genius. Now he must see you again to give it back.* "Well?" Echo asked when Maddie got to class, just a few seconds before the tardy bell rang. Maddie gave her the thumbs up and then crossed her fingers.

Jake has no idea who he's messin' with if he thinks he's going to dump me.

Mrs. Motts began the class. "Math is everything, and everything is math," she announced. She proceeded to pass out a quiz. Maddie despised math. She didn't like schoolwork in general, but math made no sense to her whatsoever. Still, she had to keep up her good grades. That was something she demanded of herself, and she didn't care how. Good thing she was sitting directly behind the most intelligent girl in the ninth grade – Grace.

Maddie smirked, thinking back to TeenScene. Boy, was she gonna have some fun messing with Grace.

Maddie tried to see around Grace's shoulders but found it impossible. The clock was ticking. Grace was speeding through the quiz. Maddie knew if she didn't act quickly, she'd be sunk. She certainly wasn't in the mood to have academic problems on top of all her other woes. She had to think of something immediately.

"Hey, Grace," Maddie whispered. "You have ... well, you have a spot on your pants." Grace stopped writing and turned around.

"What?" she asked.

"Did you ... *start*? Maddie raised her eyebrows and looked pointedly at Grace's backside. "Oh, no!" Grace took her jacket off, then stood up and hurriedly tied it around her waist. Her face was blushing red as she walked up to Mrs. Motts' desk and got a restroom pass.

Maddie squinted to make out the answers on Grace's quiz. She kept a keen eye on Mrs. Motts to make sure she didn't get caught. She was writing down the last few numbers when Grace returned.

Grace looked at Maddie, obviously bewildered. "I didn't see anything," she said, sliding back into her desk.

"When's the last time you had your eyes checked?" Maddie replied with a smirk. "You might need coke bottles ... I mean, glasses."

Grace turned back to her test as Mrs. Motts appeared beside them. "What seems to be the problem?"

Maddie shook her head. "No problem, Mrs. Motts," she answered loudly. "Grace was just asking me if she had anything on her pants."

Grace gasped and hunched even lower in her seat as everyone stared and laughed.

Maddie fumbled with the test, finished it, and

then put it on Mrs. Motts' desk. On the way back to her seat, she glanced over at Echo, who was cracking up. Maddie's heart was thumping, but she kept it cool on the outside.

*

Later that day, Maddie sat with the Scarlet Squad in the cafeteria. She was still high on her power trip from belittling Grace in math. She felt great. Strong. The Scarlet Squad was in session. If anyone at school had anything to say about the incident at the party, they didn't dare mention it in front of Maddie. Even the girls and guys at the popular table went out of their way to avoid walking past Maddie's table. No one was exempt from the Scarlet Squad's hateful stares and snide remarks.

Maddie munched on her bologna sandwich. She always acted like she loved bologna, but the truth was she hated it. Bologna was cheap. Her mother had a bad habit of drinking up the grocery money. It was nothing new, though. She had grown up with bare cupboards when her mom was on a bender.

"What's up with Jake?" Kaitlyn asked.

Maddie swallowed the last bite of her sandwich. "We're back on," she lied. "I think I was a little much for him to take in ... he underestimated me. It won't happen again."

Echo smiled. "Good boy, he catches on quick."

Maddie changed the subject. "Hey, you all need to get on TeenScene. Gran gave me a tablet for my birthday, and I got right on. It's sick."

"Whoa ... didn't know it was out yet."

"That's lit!"

"We're gonna have a little fun," Maddie smiled. "Just make a fake profile. I'm Kaylie Taylor from Cali ... yes, Taylor ... as in Jake Taylor. And you'll never in a million years believe who I'm friends with?"

"Jake?" Echo blurted.

"Heck no. Are you kiddin' me? He'd never get on social media. He barely uses his phone."

"Who?" Kaitlyn begged. "Don't leave me in suspense."

"Plain Face Grace," Maddie announced with an evil glimmer in her eye. "Oh, now that's devilishly delish."

Echo shook her head and winked. "You are *so* mean."

*

Maddie hugged her arms around her as she parted ways with Echo at the swings on their way home. The wind was icy cold. Her ears were straining for the sound of Jake's car. She hadn't seen him again all day, and he still had her purse.

She was hoping for a warm meal, even a pizza. Instead, she was greeted by a note on the kitchen table.

Don finally asked me out to dinner. Be home soon.

Maddie knew her Mom's "be home soon" meant zip. Sometimes she didn't come home at all.

She looked through the bare cupboards and came up with a peanut butter and jelly sandwich.

Pulling her tablet from the bedside drawer, Maddie silently thanked her Grandma Betty again. "You rock," she sent in an email. Her grandma was pretty mod for an old lady but wasn't on any social media platforms, resisting Maddie's numerous attempts to convince her. Grandma Betty preferred to draw or paint and was fantastic at it. She had taught Maddie to draw when she was a little girl. "You are so talented," Grandma Betty had told her. "You should at least take Art in school." But Maddie disliked anyone seeing her drawings. It made her feel naked, scared. She was afraid of being ridiculed, and the possibility of succeeding was even more uncomfortable. So, she sketched in private, occasionally sharing her work with her grandma and sister. She particularly loved drawing fashion outfits but hid the sketches in her underwear drawer. They were for her eyes only.

Logging onto TeenScene, Maddie got busy flowering up Kaylie's profile. She loved creating a whole new person. She found photos online of hot girls in skimpy bikinis and tanned guys on the beach. Kaylie had lots of friends. She also had professional parents: a nurse and a doctor.

She thought of Grace's father, the most famous

criminal attorney in Southwest Colorado, and her mother, a doctor at the hospital's chemotherapy wing. Her younger brother Gavin was as much of a geek as Grace. *I'd crawl under a rock if they were my kids.*

She studied the photos on Grace's profile. There was one from several years ago with Grace in a peachy-pink matching short set and her brother in overall shorts standing on the ledge at the Grand Canyon.

Really? Who lets their kids dress like that? Maybe their parents still dress them. Creepy either way.

There was a picture of Grace in a pink frilly dress sitting in front of a birthday cake. "Look Who's Five!" Grace had captioned the photo. Maddie remembered the party and how it was fun. They had played hide-and-go-seek for hours after eating cake. She didn't recall Grace's disgusting dress, but in those days, it didn't matter.

Who puts their baby pictures on their profile? I wouldn't ... even if I had any. Although she had seen a few of her childhood photos in Grandma Betty's picture albums, she certainly didn't have any around the house. She guessed her mom had been too wasted or absent to take pictures, and her dad sure wasn't around to take any.

Another set of pictures caught her eye in a folder named "Church." One was of Grace and Jackson when they were little. Another was of Grace being baptized into the Baptist church. Then there was a whole bunch of church camp pictures taken at a retreat on Black Bear Mountain. *Losers.*

Maddie loved snooping on Grace's page. It gave her more ammunition with which to make Grace's life a misery. She opened a folder called "Photography." She never knew Grace was an aspiring photographer. One photo was of a baby bird in a nest. "First Place!" was captioned underneath. After that, there were sunsets, sunrises, and pictures of flowers and trees.

How boring it is to be you! Where are the pictures of your friends? Oh, yeah ... you don't have any ... except Jackson, for what that's worth.

Time passed quickly as Maddie snooped Grace's page a little longer. An entire section was devoted to poetry Grace had written. So many of them had won contests.

OMG ... who writes poetry? I'll have to read these sometime ... if I can keep from puking.

There were sudden noises downstairs. Maddie bolted down the stairs to see what the commotion was all about. When she reached the kitchen, she saw her mother stumbling around. She had Maddie's cell phone in her hand. *This can't be good.*

Mom threw the phone at Maddie as hard as she could.

Maddie moved out of instinct; her phone screen smashed on the hard tile floor.

"I told you ... you are forbidden to talk to that boy." Mom's face was red, and her eyes were bloodshot. "Why is he calling you? Oh, and he left a message saying you left your purse in his car ... you are grounded for the rest of your life and don't think I won't follow through ... get your butt upstairs and don't come down until ... well ... maybe never."

Maddie couldn't believe she had left her phone on the bar where she had eaten her sandwich. And why she didn't have a lock code on it. She wanted to fight back with her mother. She was so angry. But she knew she'd never win. The best she could hope for is to make it upstairs before her mother said anything about the tablet. *Thank God for the tablet.*

"OK," Maddie managed, trying to keep the peace. She turned around and started up the stairs.

Her mom's cell phone rang. "What?"

She was silent for a minute as she listened. "We're on our way!" She turned back to Maddie. "Your sister ... she's having the baby. Get your rear in gear."

Maddie grabbed her coat and hurried to the car.

Elodie ran three red lights on the way to Pine Cove Memorial Hospital. Maddie was accustomed to it. She couldn't count the number of wrecks her mother had when she was a little girl. There were other times she would have wrecked if Maddie hadn't grabbed the wheel. It was a skill Ashley had taught her just in case their mother passed out while driving.

They reached the hospital in record time.

In the maternity ward, Ashley was covered in sweat.

"Good, you're here," Samuel said. "I'm gonna go get some dinner."

Once Samuel left, Ashley began to talk when the pains eased. "I called his work when I went into labor, Mad."

Maddie drew closer, holding her sister's hand.

"He doesn't even work there anymore ... he was fired weeks ago." Maddie was furious. She'd deal with Samuel later.

"I think he's been cheating on me. Why else would he be lying about everything?"

"Breathe, Ash ... it's all about you ... and Baby Liam ... we'll get through this." Maddie's heart clenched when she saw Ashley in so much pain. "We've gotten through everything life's thrown at us so far, and we did it ... together. So come on now; you can do it."

Mom burst through the doors, followed by a nurse. The nurse looked at the monitor and frowned.

"We've got to get you into the delivery room," she said with an urgency in her voice. She buzzed the doctor and wheeled Ashley's bed out of the room.

"I love you, sissy!" Maddie felt like the biggest part of her heart was being ripped out of her chest. She watched the nurses' back disappear down the sterile hallway. All they could do now was wait. Maddie went in search of a vending machine, anything to get away from Elodie, who had started ranting about Samuel, Ashley, and other family members. When she was like this, Maddie knew it was best to be as far away as possible.

She sat in a small waiting room, sipping her soda and thinking of the anguish on Ashley's face when she heard a familiar voice coming from the reception desk.

"I'm here to see my grandfather, Earl Taylor," Jake said. He was breathless and panicked. Maddie ducked back out of the hallway, knowing it was better that way ... for the moment, at least. She was coming up with a plan.

SEVEN

Maddie was dying to hold the baby again. He was as cute as a button, soft and warm – so innocent and pure. Last night – had it only been last night? – was crazy. Ashley had an emergency delivery. Baby Liam was fine, but thanks to the drama and the pain medication, Ashley accidentally let something slip to Mom about Samuel. Mom then flipped out, screamed at Samuel, and they both ended up being escorted out by security.

Maddie had sat with Ashley in recovery until she was transferred back to the ward and had just stepped out to call Grandma Betty to give her the good news and let Ash sleep for a bit. Grandma Betty promised to bring cookies – lots of cookies. Maddie remembered how her grandma's cookies used to make everything better. She wished they still could.

She was heading back to Ash's room, completely exhausted when she came face to face with Jake.

"Oh crap!"

Jake looked puzzled. "Crap? That's a heck of a greeting."

"I ... well, I just look like crap," she corrected, running a finger through her tangled hair. Jake smiled. "Nah, you look fine. What are you doing here, though?"

"My sister just had a baby." Jake nodded. "Congrats."

"I'm sorry. How rude of me. What are you doing here?"

"My grandpa had a heart attack." Jake's face was tight. "They think he'll be OK ... but I'm not sure. I can't lose him. He's the best grandpa ever."

Maddie found herself being drawn in even though she didn't want to feel sorry for him. She tried to come across as cool, detached. Maddie couldn't imagine what it would be like to lose Grandma Betty. It was something she had worried about ever since she was a little girl. When she was in seventh grade, Grandma Betty had stopped by the house one Sunday for pizza. Mom was plastered as usual and started to argue with her. Grandma Betty started having chest pains, so Maddie called the ambulance and rushed with her to the hospital. She was scared but would do anything to save her grandmother.

Remember how he left you stranded at your party. Remember how he tried to dump you.

"I have your purse in my car," Jake added. "I tried to call you. I've just gotta run back to the room to grab my keys but do you want to meet me in the parking lot in five?"

"Sure, Jake." She smiled. Maybe she'd get a hug from him out there or kiss him on the lips. Perhaps they'd even go for a drive. This could turn out to be a great day.

She swung back into Ashley's room and did a double-take. Samuel was standing over the baby.

"What are *you* doing here?"

"Maddie!" Ash was awake.

"What's he doing here? Do you want me to call security again?"

"It's OK," Ashley sighed. "Samuel came by to see the baby. We were talking ..."

"He's my son," Samuel said. "You can't just kick me out of here." He stepped into the adjacent restroom.

Maddie plopped down on a chair beside her sister's bed. "Aren't you leaving him? After all the lies?"

Ashley looked at Liam in his bassinet and then at Maddie. "If we can make it work, we have to ... for his sake."

Maddie took a deep breath. She couldn't deal with this right now. She needed to get her purse off Jake, get home, see if her phone was working, check her social media and get some sleep. "Whatever, Ash. But I think you should come home and raise the baby there. Without him. I can babysit, you know."

Ashley smiled softly and reached over to pat Maddie's leg. "I know ... we'll see how it goes." Maddie gave the baby a peck on the cheek and hugged her sister. "I'm gonna walk home," she said.

"Thank you for being here for me, Mad. We love you."

Maddie made her way out to the parking lot. There was Jake's car – hard to miss. And there was Jake, leaning on it. But who was the girl leaning against him? Talking closely with him? Did he have his arm around her? Chloe. What is going on?

I can't breathe.

Maddie felt every inch of her being sink into nothingness. Inside she felt alone and forgotten, betrayed to the point of sheer physical pain. It was an old, familiar feeling. It felt like knives piercing her heart.

She approached them, feeling like she was outside her body. Jake handed her the purse. "Slut," Maddie heard herself say to Chloe. She was numb.

"Maddie, get a grip!" Jake stepped forward, almost protecting Chloe from her. He was angrier than she'd ever seen him.

Maddie turned and left. She was halfway home before realizing she was shaking. What the hell just happened? Since when had Jake and Chloe been together? Why her? She had struggled with Chloe since the first grade. She was never sure if Chloe liked her or not. Chloe was friendly to her face, but Maddie was always left out when she was around Isabella and Jasmine. And then there was the flirting incident at the Ice Hut at Maddie's party.

She was almost home.

"Hey, Maddie!" SJ was walking down the sidewalk towards her, holding hands with Kyle the Pile. Arkadia and Chad were also holding hands behind them.

Oh, great. Maddie's face felt like plastic when she tried to stretch it into a smile. Her hair was greasy. She needed a shower.

"Can you believe Chloe's gone straight for your sloppy seconds?" Arkadia laughed. "We saw her and Jake cruising around."

Maddie was furious and devastated at the same time. She couldn't believe Jake and Chloe were flaunting themselves all over town.

"Oh, Maddie, thanks for setting us up, by the way," SJ said. "Kyle's gonna come over and meet my parents, so we've gotta take off."

Ew. Maddie couldn't believe her mean antics had backfired and turned into an apparent match made in heaven. *They weren't meant actually to like each other.*

"You guys use protection, OK?" Maddie stabbed. "I'm coming from the hospital. Ash just had a baby."

SJ turned bright red. "Maddie!" Arkadia exclaimed.

"Serious," Maddie said. "It happens." She crossed the street and headed down the sidewalk to her house.

*

Mom wasn't home, thank God. Maddie picked up her smashed phone off the floor. It felt like a million years since Mom had thrown it at her. She plugged it in, but the screen was impossible to read.

I wonder what it's like to want to be around your mom or, even better, for your mom to want to be around you.

She knew she should be hungry but thinking of Jake and Chloe made her stomach hurt. There was nothing in the fridge, anyway.

It seemed like everyone had someone ... except for her. Ash had Liam now, and it sounded like she was going to stick with Samuel. Chad and Arkadia, Kyle and SJ, and now Jake and Chloe. Echo had her lovely family. Even Grace had Jackson. It annoyed Maddie how he protected Grace in his own weird way. Would anyone protect Maddie like that?

She went up to her room, kissed Shadow, pulled out her tablet, and clicked onto TeenScene. Her head was kind of spinning – how many hours had she been awake now? But she had to check-in with her socials. First, she brought Echo, Kaitlyn, and Sophia up to date on the recent events: her phone was history, Ashley had her baby, and she had dumped Jake.

Then she logged into Kaylie's profile and checked to see if Grace was online.

Of course, she is. What else does she have to do except homework or write poetry?

Kaylie: hey, chica. Sup?

Grace: Not much. I just finished reading "The Grapes of Wrath" for English Lit. Good book. Highly recommend.

Kaylie: u sure sound smart

Grace: I try. Lol.

Kaylie: bet the guys dig that

Grace: Not really. Jackson thinks it's cool. But he's not my boyfriend. Just a friend. My not- boyfriend. Lol. I'm not sure what the other guys think. It doesn't matter. I'm just me.

Kaylie: so who's ur crush?

Grace: He's already got a girlfriend.

Kaylie: don't let that stop u, lol

Grace: I just think he's cute, that's all. He's totally taken. He was with a really mean girl named Maddie. Now he's with the most popular girl in school, Chloe. She's gorgeous, so not a chance he'd like me. Besides, I don't want a bf. I just think he's a nice guy and that he's cute.

Maddie wanted to fly through the tablet screen. She'd assumed Grace would have a crush on some nerdy church guy. She had the sudden urge to beat the living daylights out of her.

Grace has a crush on Jake. *How dare she! And how does she even know about Chloe and Jake? Am I that out of touch?*

With a deep breath, Maddie began to type, her hands still trembling from her emotional outburst.

Kaylie: so, if u cld go out with anyone in the world, who wld it be?

Grace: Jake Taylor.

I've got her now. Maddie screenshot Grace's admission and filed it on her tablet in a folder she named "Homework."

Kaylie: he sounds like a dream

Grace: Lol. A dream with eyes of green. That's how the poem goes.

Kaylie: poem?

Grace: Yes. I write poetry.

Kaylie: can u send that poem? i'd love to read it

Grace: That one's top secret. No offense. I gotta get my poetry notebook out of my backpack. I'll send a diff one.

Kaylie: NP

But there *was* a problem. Maddie was burning with rage. Jake was hers. Or, at least, he used to be. She hated Grace more than ever.

Kaylie: i've got a friend with green eyes. hayden. how bout i hook u up with him?

Grace: I don't know. I don't feel comfortable talking to boys except for Jackson.

Kaylie: is that jackson & u on ur profile pic?

Grace: He's, my BFF. We've been friends all our lives. His father is the pastor of my family church. This is my favorite picture of us.

Maddie stared at the photo. It was Grace and Jackson beside a campfire in the mountains. Jackson was strumming a guitar, and it looked like they were both singing.

Oh my god, talk about kum-ba-yah! I imagine you two had the wolves howling.

Grace: That was at a church camp in Aspen. It was so much fun!

Kaylie: sweet! u go 2 church?

Grace: Yes. I love our church. There are some wonderful people in the church.

Kaylie: i never liked church myself. 2 judgmental

Grace: Oh, ours isn't like that. We welcome everyone. That's one of the things I love about going to church.

Liar! Your family kicked us out.

Kaylie: gotta go. i'll have hayden send u a friend request. TTYL

Grace: OK. TTYL.

Right away, Maddie got busy creating a profile for Hayden. Hometown: San Diego, just like Kaylie. Brown hair, green eyes, tall, dark, and handsome. She needed a profile picture and found an ideal one – a California dude surfing. It was perfect.

Maddie's tablet dinged. Grace had sent a poem to Kaylie. Maddie downloaded it and began to read it:

My Happy Place

There is a place, way up high -

Where the mountain top kisses the sky

I've only been there a couple of times

But I revisit often in my mind.

It's a peaceful solace where time stands still

With a blue lake and mountain cave

My heart is happy as I look down.

I refresh my soul high above the town.

No worries. No cares can ever find me there.

A smile graces my face

For I am in ... my happy place.

OMG ... I want to vomit! Only you could have a happy place like that.

Poetry notebook, indeed. Maddie pulled out her pad and began to sketch with random strokes. Adrenaline pumped through her veins, thinking of the possibilities that lay ahead. When she was through, she realized she had drawn her version of Grace's happy place.

Maddie sent a friend request to Grace under Hayden's name. Once again, Grace's acceptance came immediately.

Pathetic, she has no life.

Hayden: Hey, thanks for friending me.

Grace: NP. A friend of Kaylie's is a friend of mine.

Hayden: Your profile pic is cute.

Grace: Thanks. Yours is cool. I wish I could surf. But I live in Colorado.

Hayden: I love the mountains. Do you snow ski?

Grace: Yes. I go skiing with my family a lot.

A streak of jealousy zipped through Maddie. She didn't know Grace skied. Even though Pine Cove was less than an hour away from one of the world's best ski resorts, she had never been skiing. If she had a real family and money, maybe she would ski too.

Hayden: Maybe I'll have to come and check the mountains out sometime. My parents just bought a winter house in Telluride. You anywhere around there?

Grace: I live very close to Telluride.

Hayden: We'll be up there at Christmas. Maybe we can meet up?

Grace: I'm not allowed to go out unchaperoned. I'm just 14.

Hayden: I just turned 16 and got a car yesterday, so I'm ready to take a road trip. NP on parents. I'll take them with us.

Grace: Sweet!

Maddie was startled by her bedroom door flying open. Mom. Maddie made a quick swipe of her finger and pulled up a math app.

Mom exploded. "NO ELECTRONICS!"

"But Mom, I'm doing schoolwork ... see?" She held up the math page. "Grandma had it set up for school."

Elodie seemed satisfied with the lie. "Get to bed soon," she ordered and closed the bedroom door.

Maddie was tired after all. She fell asleep, counting ways to get her hands on Grace's poem. She already knew exactly what she was going to do with it, and she couldn't wait.

EIGHT

Two weeks of being grounded flew by, mainly because Maddie was so wrapped up in giving Grace, Chloe, and Jackson a hard time. Maddie bombarded all the socials with her comments and thoughts of the three of them. Grace aka Plain Face Grace, who wears the thickest glasses in school. No-action Jackson was a nerd and wimp. Only Grace would disagree, and she was such a scaredy-cat she would not dare post a reply.

Chloe is a slut, constantly flinging herself at so many boys. Better watch your boyfriends! Anyone who responded disagreeing with Maddie also felt her wrath. Game on.

She was still torn up about Jake and Chloe, but Grace served as the perfect target for Maddie's hatred. Maddie was on a mission and couldn't have stopped even if she'd wanted to. Plain Face Grace, what a Dis-Grace, who can challenge that comment. Not even Jackson stood up for her when Maddie posted it on her page for all to see and tagged Grace.

It's true, plain face, terrible clothes, no personality. Who would want Grace for a friend?

It was the last day of school before Thanksgiving break, the day of the school talent show. Grace had worn a pair of ugly pink overalls to school. Maddie couldn't let it slide in math. "Wearin' those digs to the hoedown tonight?" Maddie inquired in a whisper from her seat behind Grace's.

"Uh, no, right after school, I'm going to help my mom plant flowers at the hospital. Then I'll change into my dress."

"Jake goin' with ya?" Maddie slipped up. She never meant to mention that she knew about Jake. "No ... Jackson is," Grace replied, wrinkling her nose. "I haven't ever spoken to Jake."

"Oh, OK. Must be a rumor," Maddie grinned. "Don't worry. I won't tell Chloe." Grace turned back around, away from Maddie.

Maddie looked down at Grace's open backpack sitting where it always did – on the floor right in front of her feet. Usually, it bothered Maddie to no end. But today, she was glad it was there. She dropped a pen, and when leaning down to pick it up, she snagged a floral notebook out of Grace's backpack. Slowly and methodically, she opened it further with her foot until she could see the contents inside. Bingo. Then, with one swift, sneaky move, she stuffed it into her backpack.

Boom! I hope that is her poem book! How could it

not be with all those sickening daisies all over it?

Mrs. Motts told the class to get started on their homework and left the room. Maddie couldn't help it. She wrote a note that read: "You *and* your clothes are ugly." She folded it up and chucked it onto Grace's desk.

Suddenly, there was a hand ... Mrs. Motts' hand. *Where did SHE come from?*

Mrs. Motts took the note from Grace, uncrumpled it, and read it to herself. "I will need to speak to you at the end of the day in Mr. Freeman's office," she said sternly, dark eyes peering through her bifocals.

"Yes, Mrs. Motts," Maddie said with a slight nod and the saddest eyes she could muster.

*

Maddie couldn't wait to be surrounded by the girls at their spot in the cafeteria. "Can you believe I'm in trouble for talking to Plain Face?"

"Talking to her?" Echo questioned. "I bet you were *talking* to her."

"Somebody's gotta talk to her," Maddie said. "Nobody else does, poor thang."

Kaitlyn gave a head-point across the lunchroom. Maddie turned and looked. It was Jake and Chloe.

"Yikes," Sophia commented under her breath. "Big yikes," Kaitlyn returned.

He never once ate lunch with me.

"Who cares?" Maddie commented, turning her

back on the couple. "She's just doin' it to try to make me jealous, but soon she'll see that I don't care."

Sophia let out a laugh. "I can't tell."

Maddie squinted her eyes. She was furious. "Who are you going to the talent contest with tonight, anyway? Kaitlyn? You know, people are starting to wonder about you two."

Sophia didn't bite. Maddie knew none of the girls wanted to get in a fight with her right now. Still, she couldn't help picking at them.

"You and Chad going to the talent show?" Maddie asked Arkadia. "You should do your disappearing act."

"What disappearing act?" Arkadia asked.

"The one you're going to do if you keep putting Chad above your loyalty to the group," Maddie said.

Arkadia looked nervous and didn't answer.

"Yeah, actually, I've decided I want to see that act," Maddie said. "Don't hang around us anymore. If we want to see you or talk to you, we'll let you know." She motioned for Arkadia to shoo away and, like a whipped dog, Arkadia obediently left the table.

Echo, Kaitlyn, and Sophia didn't say a word. They were noticeably stunned at what Maddie had said.

The next few hours seemed to take a lifetime to pass. When the last bell rang, Maddie headed to Mr. Freeman's office. She put on the most somber face she could. It was only one note – surely, she couldn't get in too much trouble. But still. She prided herself on being stealthy. Today she'd been sloppy to get caught out.

Mr. Freeman met her in the lobby outside his office wearing a tie covered in turkeys. He had a tie for every holiday. *So lame.* Mrs. Motts was already there. The office was as stale as the principal, with two stiff wooden chairs and a way-too-tidy oak desk. On his wall hung a picture of him and his wife, with a big brown dog.

Figures. Dog people have no class.

"Maddison, I am quite aware that you are nasty to Grace Harwood regularly," Mrs. Motts began. "And it must stop."

Mr. Freeman was perched behind his desk, observing. "Yes, Maddison. At Pine Cove High, bullying will not be tolerated. Understood?"

"Yes, sir," Maddie said in a small, low voice.

"If there is another incident, we will not only suspend you and inform your mother. We will have to report it to the authorities," Mrs. Motts went on. "And trust me, you do not want me to do that."

"No, ma'am."

"Then we are trusting you have learned your lesson, young lady," Mr. Freeman concluded. "Have a good Thanksgiving break."

Maddie nodded and walked out of the office into the lobby. She headed down the deserted hallway and made it out the side door. Where were the girls?

Maddie couldn't believe they didn't wait for her. She expected more loyalty than that from Echo, at least.

As she walked across the teachers' parking lot, Mr. Freeman was getting in his silver Cadillac.

"Make good choices!" he called. She gave him her sweetest smile.

*

The minute she got home, Maddie ran to her room and pulled the daisy notebook from her backpack. It was titled "A Patchwork of Poems."

YES!

She flicked through the handwritten pages. There was one poem called "Green Eyed Dream." She skimmed it, a smile growing bigger at each line. This was better than expected.

But no time to gloat. She had to get ready for the talent show. She already had a red top picked out to go with her favorite jeans. She had swiped a pair of new boots at Striplings the last time she went by, pretending to visit her mother. They were perfect with her outfit. Lip gloss was all she needed to complete her look.

On the way out, Mom came in the front door like a tornado. *If only I had got ready quicker, I could have missed her by seconds.*

"Where do you think *you're* going?" Mom asked, looking her up and down.

Maddie was worried. She never knew what mood to expect from her mother. "The Thanksgiving talent show at school," she answered. "You said I could go, remember?"

Mom poured a drink of vodka and tonic. "No, I don't." Maddie wasn't beyond pleading. She simply *had* to go.

"You said if I made an A in math, I could go," Maddie reminded. "And I did." Mom's mouth fell into a frown. "I didn't see no report card."

Maddie shook her head in frustration. "Mom ... you signed it." Mom thought about it for a minute. "Oh. Well then, OK." Maddie had signed her own report card.

"If I catch you with that junior, I'll pull you out of the talent show by your ear, and you'll be grounded for life," Elodie threatened.

Maddie laughed. "Jake's a loser. So, you don't have to worry about him. And you can only ground me until I'm eighteen cuz then, I'm like ... outta here."

"Promise?"

"About Jake?" Maddie asked. "Yes."

"No. About moving out."

"Oh yeah," Maddie replied without a second thought. "I promise!" Elodie headed to the sofa.

Maddie snuck a knife from the kitchen drawer and slid it into her purse. "Love!" she called to her mom out of habit. It was something they had said back and forth since she was a little girl. She heard the TV click on.

The sun was beginning to set, and it was chilly out, but Maddie's heart was pounding so hard she barely noticed. Echo was waiting on the swing at the park.

"How'd it go with Tie Face?" Echo asked.

"Better than he realizes," she replied. "If he thinks he can call me out like that ..."

"Yeah, he's just the principal," Echo giggled. "No match for my Maddie."

The two hurried through the park, down the sidewalk, and across the parking lot to the school gym.

Maddie took pleasure in the heads that turned when she walked into the gym. The gym was decorated in a festive Thanksgiving theme, compliments of the Student Council, who set up a makeshift stage with spotlights and a microphone. In addition, an outdated slide projector was set up to shine onto a screen on the wall, just like Mr. Freeman had told them in the initial contest announcement. "You can show pictures or use it as part of your act."

Oh, I've got something to show ... Maddie carefully scoped out how it was all set up.

It took less than a minute to spot Jake and Chloe. They were already taking their seats. It infuriated Maddie that Chloe looked gorgeous. She was the athletic type – she had been a cheerleader ever since Maddie could remember. Maddie wished for Chloe's curves.

"There's our Scarlet Squad." Echo pulled Maddie

across the crowded gym to the refreshment table where Sophia and Kaitlyn waited. Arkadia was behaving, sitting a few rows away with Chad.

"Hey, Scarlets!" Sophia said.

Kaitlyn shot a smile their way too.

"Your BFF is right over there ... with her not-boyfriend," Sophia said. "Don't they look adorable?"

Sure enough, Grace was sitting in the corner wearing a blue and green plaid dress. She wore leggings underneath, no doubt her mother's idea in case her legs got cold or showed too much skin. Grace's face was as plain as ever. *Not even lipgloss, seriously she doesn't even try to look nice.*

It made Maddie angry that Grace had all the resources to have clothes in style, or at least that weren't two decades out of date. Her parents made good money. They had a big house in the most prestigious development in town, Gateway. But no ... she chose to be an eyesore.

Milton Black, another nobody in their year, walked up to get refreshments from the table. Maddie elbowed Echo.

"My friend thinks you're hot," Maddie told him. "She wants to connect the dots on your freckle face."

Maddie and Echo burst out laughing. Milton left without a snack or a drink.

Mr. Freeman walked onto the stage and welcomed everyone to the talent show. "You are in store for a lot of fun tonight," he said.

Everyone's attention was on the principal. As he was speaking, Maddie took the poem from her purse, wrote something on it, and casually made her way to the overhead projector in the corner of the room. She slipped it on the glass slide and walked back to take a seat with the Scarlet Squad.

"Now, I would like for our Class President of the Senior Class, Tanner Miller, to say a few words and read the program. This will outline the order of talents that will be performing tonight," Mr. Freeman said. The Class President walked up to the stage, took the microphone, and read the screen.

"This goes out to Jake Taylor. 'Green-Eyed Dream,' by Grace Harwood."

Maddie saw Grace stiffen with shock. She looked like she didn't know whether to sink into the floor or make a run for the door. Jackson was whispering to her.

Tanner looked a bit confused but kept reading.

Love from afar

You do not see me standing here. You do not feel my breath so near

If only one day you turned to see the loving glance you'd get from me

But what would I do if you looked my way?

Would I smile at you or run away?

Oh, why is love so hard to grasp

And how on earth do you make it last?

Maybe it's safer to watch from afar and continue to wish upon a star

And then to dream my perfect dream about a boy with eyes of green

A dull roar built up in the gym as everyone began to clamor, call out, and wolf whistle about the poem. Way too soon for Maddie's liking, Mr. Freeman walked to the projector and corrected the paper on the glass.

"I'm not sure where that fell into the mix, but ... thank you, Grace, beautiful poem. And now ... I see ... actually, Grace and Jackson are first up."

Jackson led Grace to the stage. She looked like a pathetic little mouse, eyes wide. Maddie couldn't believe she was going to go ahead with whatever stupid act they'd planned. After that poem – in front of everyone – how embarrassing. Maddie would rather die.

Jackson picked up a guitar and began to strum. Grace started to sing "Amazing Grace" in a small, shaky voice. Echo, Kaitlyn, and Sophia laughed.

Does she not know what a fool she's making of herself?

Jackson joined in the song. Grace's voice became stronger and stronger until she belted out the words in the most angelic voice Maddie had ever heard. To her disgust, it sounded good. There was some distant memory in the back of Maddie's mind: people singing together. Beautiful music. Her heart was swelling, feeling nice, safe. She felt her throat tighten and clenched her fists to stop tears from building in her eyes.

When the song was over, the gym roared. "Encore ... Encore!"

Grace smiled and sang the chorus once more. Finally, she ended with a bow and walked off the stage with the entire school cheering.

"Amazing Grace! Amazing Grace!" the kids were chanting.

Maddie saw Jake standing and cheering. She needed air. She pushed past the Scarlets and snuck out the side door. A cold wind was blowing. The parking lot was dim except for the faint light of a half-moon, but it was easy to spot Jake's Mustang. She had to be quick and quiet. She slid the knife out of her purse and pushed it into the front tire with one slick, smooth move. She pulled the knife out and felt the tire begin to deflate.

Hearing footsteps, she skirted between the rows of cars. If she could make it across the graveled parking lot, she could hide in the bushes that outlined the school. She'd be safely out of sight then. But getting there was risky.

The footsteps stopped. Maddie saw a silhouette

of a couple embracing. She knew it was Jake and Chloe. They were kissing. She wanted to puke, but she also wanted to fall into his arms. "Oh crap," Jake said. "I've got a flat."

Maddie had to get out of there. She shuffled backward in a crouch, the gravel crunching beneath her boots. Standing straight, she started running, rounding the corner, her feet skidding right out from under her. She could hear voices. They were coming. They were going to see her any moment. She was going to jail if she didn't get up and go. She pulled herself to her feet and flew down the sidewalk, across the pitch-black park, down the street to her house. For the first time that she could ever remember, she couldn't wait to get home.

NINE

T hank God it was Thanksgiving break. Had she not been off school for the week, she was sure she would have been busted for the tire episode. She really wanted to take a rest from her bad behavior - only because she was worried she'd get caught. Her heart was still pumping from the near disaster in the parking lot. But being bad was the only thing that made her feel better.

Maddie was bored. Luckily Mom seemed to be out all week, so Maddie passed the hours on her tablet. Although she rarely posted under her own name, being Kaylie and Hayden was strangely soothing. It was exciting being from sunny California.

Grace really believed she had Californian friends online. The dumb girl had no earthly idea.

Kaylie: so what do u think about hayden?

Grace: He's nice ... and cute.

Kaylie: i hear he digs u. lucky to be u

Grace: I hope he does.

Kaylie: i'm going to a party tonight, so i gotta jam. just wanted to check in with u. u no ur one of my gt girls now

Grace: gt?

Kaylie: go-to girls. it's like a bunch of bffs. gotta teach u some cali slang. i gotta net now, but we'll get u schooled sapa

Grace: Net? Sapa?

Kaylie: omg girl. net means like gotta go. and sapa: soon as possible airhead!

Grace: OK

Kaylie: TTYL eggie!

Grace: Eggie?

Kaylie: yass ... like an eggcellent friend

Grace: OK. TTYL eggie!

Maddie was rolling on the bed, laughing so hard her sides ached. *Net. Sapa. Eggie.* She couldn't wait to tell the Scarlet Squad.

The house was empty except for the soft purrs of her beloved Shadow. But Shadow could only offer so much company. She had to find something to keep her busy.

I think I'll go see Baby Liam. She had only visited once since Ashley had brought him home from the hospital. Seeing Samuel and Ashley playing happy families together was more than she could bear. *What*

does she see in him?

On the way to Ashley's apartment, Maddie passed by Chloe's house. She had been there once, years ago, for a slumber party. At first, she had felt lucky for being invited to the A-list event, but as the night went on, she realized none of the girls liked her. She was the last to be picked when they chose teams for games they played. She heard some of the girls whispering and was sure they were gossiping about her. Things got so bad, she tried to call her mom to come to get her, but Elodie wasn't home ... of course.

After the sleepover fiasco, Maddie stopped dreaming of becoming one of the popular girls. Soon after, she created her group – the Scarlet Squad, named after her favorite color. She based it on a movie about girls like her who were really good at being bad. With Echo, Kaitlyn, Sophia, and sometimes Arkadia on board, she had the power to make lives miserable. She could have her revenge, making kids pay for their wrongs or just pick on people for the thrill of it.

She enjoyed her position as leader of the pack. It was a lot more rewarding than being popular. She'd gladly settle for being well known and feared.

As Maddie passed by Chloe's house, she noted the manicured lawn and a new game and media bungalow. Where Maddie had heard Chloe and her siblings hosted parties and sleepovers.

Maddie didn't care that she had never been invited to one. She did wonder what it would be like to have parents like Chloe's, though. Why was it that

Chloe had everything ... including Jake?

A dog with long golden hair followed her down the fence line, barking annoyingly. Maddie took a quick look around the empty street, then quickly opened the gate. The stupid dog jumped at Maddie, smearing slobber over her hand, then took off across the street. *I hope it gets lost and doesn't come back. Chloe deserves to have something she loved taken away from her. An eye for an eye.*

She rounded the corner and saw three girls walking towards her, holding the dog by the collar. Chloe, Isabella, and Jasmine. There was no way to avoid them, so Maddie kept walking. As she tried to pass them, the dog pulled away from Chloe and jumped its dirty feet up onto Maddie's shirt, licking her. Maddie shrieked and pushed it away. *Disgusting.*

"Goldie, get down!"

"She acts like she recognizes her," Maddie heard Isabella say. "I bet *she's* the one that let her out!"

"Your dog is as out of control as you are," Maddie spat at Chloe.

Ten minutes later, Maddie was at Ash's apartment. Ash was feeding Liam on the couch. The place was trashed. Clothes and laundry everywhere, dirty dishes piled in the kitchen. It was so messy Maddie couldn't breathe.

"Doesn't Samuel help with any of this?" Maddie asked Ash, gesturing around the apartment as she started tidying.

Ash just shook her head tiredly. "He's barely ever

here," she said.

"Are you kidding me? Why haven't you told me? I still think you need to come home, Ash." Ashley sighed. "It's not that easy, sis," she began. "Mom is ... Mom. She interferes with everything. I don't want her trying to raise Baby Liam. I want to stick it out here. But I must get a job. I do have a lead ... being a bartender."

"You can't be a bartender," Maddie raged as she began to mop. "You have a baby!"

"Mom did!" Ashley argued. Realizing what she had said, she shook her head. "Yeah ... guess you're right."

Maddie looked down at Liam. He was so tiny, so precious. She never wanted him to go through what she and her sister had gone through.

*

After a couple of hours of OCD cleaning Ash's apartment, Maddie took off. She decided to take the scenic route home: two miles out of the way past Pine Cove's outskirts, over by the lake. She was sure she knew where Jake lived. She hoped he'd be home.

It was growing dark and cold by the time Maddie got to Jake's parents' hemp farm. She was exhausted, hungry, and freezing, but she wanted to see where he lived and if he was home. She stayed in the tree line close to the house.

The family was eating together at the dinner table. Warm light spilled out of the window. Maddie pictured herself sitting with them, eating something hot and delicious, maybe holding hands with Jake under the table.

Then a third figure appeared. Chloe. Maddie's dreamy vision was shattered. Jake needed to pay.

Maddie crept to Jake's parked Mustang. She took out her keys from her purse and scratched them along the side of the car several times. *Not so "red hot" now, Jake, are you?*

TEN

It was Sunday, Elodie's day off from the department store. Maddie woke up obnoxiously early and was ready to get out of the house the minute she did. She hated being at home with her mother.

She took a quick shower, threw on a Pine Cove High sweatshirt she had helped herself to from the lost and found bin in the gymnasium and bolted downstairs. Maddie hoped her mom was still in bed sleeping off the hangover she likely had from her late night out. The coast looked clear, so she hurried to the kitchen to write a note saying she'd be home later.

"Excuse me, lit'l lady. Going somewhere?"

"Mornin', Mom. I was going over to have breakfast with Echo and her mom ... if that's all right with you?" Maddie forced an endearing smile and kiss to her mother's cheek.

Mom adored Echo's mother, Lexie. The two had become friends years ago before the girls were even in kindergarten.

"At their house?"

"Yes, you know how Lexie loves to cook. I can give Echo a call and see if you can come along. I'm sure Lexie would love you to visit." Maddie knew Mom would want no part of an alcohol- free breakfast.

"I think I'll pass," she replied, mixing up a Bloody Mary to start the day with. "I've got a big night tonight ... a date with a new eligible bachelor in town, Ben Kirby. He's quite the catch! He's from Texas. And, incidentally, if things go well, I'll be in very late tonight ... *if* I come in at all." She shot a wink Maddie's way.

Gross.

A scene from *Girls Will Be Girls* flashed in Maddie's mind. "Hey, Mom, do you mind if the girls spend the night? You know, to keep me company. It gets lonely without you here."

Elodie frowned. Her painted eyebrows furrowed, and her lips grew tight. "Oh, I dunno about that, Mad ... how many girls and who are they?"

"Just Echo, Kaitlyn, Sophia, and maybe ... if she's lucky ... Arkadia. That's all. We could order a pizza or somethin' ... you don't have to do anything except go on your hot date and have a good time. And, if you don't make it in ... no biggie. We'll be fine." Maddie knew just how to play her mother. Sometimes it was convenient to have a drunk for a mom.

"Well, guess it can't hurt anything," Elodie conceded. "Tell Lexie I said we have to catch up soon."

Maddie gave her mother another hug and flew out the door before she changed her mind. It was only ten-thirty. She was sure Echo wasn't up yet. She liked to sleep until noon whenever she had the chance. Maddie had some time to kill, so she wandered over towards Chloe's. Maybe she'd get an opportunity to let Goldie out again, this time without interference.

Living in a remote mountain town did have its perks, and beauty was one of them. The sun was out, there was no wind, so it was warmer than usual even though it was fall. The crisp leaves were in vibrant colors of gold, red and yellow. Most years, it was already snowing before Thanksgiving, but this year was the warmest it had been in decades, which was something Maddie didn't mind at all. She was never fond of the cold.

She arrived at Chloe's fence. *Darn ... Goldie isn't out in the yard.*

A panel truck pulled up from behind, startling Maddie. She hoped desperately it wasn't Chloe. She turned around and saw that the side of the truck read "Pine Cove Florist."

"Good morning. Are you Chloe?" the delivery man called.

I wish.

"It depends," she said after a second.

The driver held out a beautiful bouquet of fall flowers carefully arranged in a festive ceramic pumpkin vase.

"Oh ... how lovely," she exclaimed, taking the flowers. "I wonder who they're from." She looked at the tag and smiled. "My boyfriend ... Jake ... he is soo precious!"

After he drove off, Maddie whipped a u-turn and took off the way she had come. She had to get to Echo's house, even if it meant waking her up. No way could she get caught with the goods. She thought of the rose on her birthday. No one had ever given her flowers before. These flowers should have been for her.

It didn't take long to get to Echo's house. She knocked on the door. Echo's mother, Lexie, answered with a big smile.

"Oh my, what gorgeous flowers!"

Maddie held them out to her. "They're for you. Happy Thanksgiving!"

"Aren't you a sweetheart? Won't you come in?"

Lexie had always been Maddie's idea of a model mom. She always helped at school and then became a homeroom mother in Echo and Maddie's earlier years at Pine Cove Elementary. When those days ended, she became an even cooler mom – taking them to the mall several towns away and joining them in gossip sessions. And she cooked. She did all the things Maddie's mom never did.

In Echo's room, Maddie filled her in about the flowers.

"OMG ... and you gave them to my mom?" Echo

asked, cracking up. "You are cray-cray ... but ... in a good way!"

Lexie called the girls out to lunch. Something smelled so good.

Echo's older brother, Elmo, burst through the front door and joined them. "How's it goin', Mad?" he asked with a slap on her shoulder. "You turn fourteen and think you're too good to come around or what?"

Elmo would kill her if he knew half of what she had been doing. He was like the brother she'd never had.

"Nope ... just trying to avoid you. You stink like a bear or something," Maddie teased, wafting her hand. He was an outdoorsy guy.

"Well, you won't have to worry about that after vacation," Elmo fired back. "I'm off to Montana to lead some survival classes."

Lexie delivered sizzling hot grilled cheese sandwiches and fried pickles to the table.

"We miss our second daughter!" Maddie's father, Mike, laughed as he dug into his sandwich. "Elmo will be living in the woods, you know. I hear trees like to spend a lot of time on the computer. Do you know how they get online?"

Maddie shrugged her shoulders. "No. How?"

"They log in!" Mike roared.

Echo rolled her eyes. "Dad ... stop!"

"Why don't skeletons have cell phones?" Mike

continued. "I dunno," Maddie answered.

"Because they don't have anybody to talk to ... get it? No body?" Mike was laughing hysterically at his own joke.

"Dad, please!"

Mike smirked. "OK ... but in all seriousness, all my son had to do to get accepted into MIT was cough."

Elmo stopped chewing for a minute, "What?"

"Oh ... *hack*, I mean."

Now Elmo rolled his eyes. "It's true ... along with good grades and a near-perfect entrance test, I had to hack into a social media account. It didn't matter which one, so I chose that new teen one ... it was stupid easy, though, because you don't even need a code to break into someone's account. You just put in 'XXX.' And, if you girls so much as think about getting on there, I'll skin you. It's not a safe place at all ... but it did help get me into MIT."

What? XXX? Maddie couldn't wait to get to her tablet. Elmo had just changed her life forever ... and Grace's too. She tried to hide her enthusiasm, but it wasn't easy. She was already making plans for the evening ahead.

*

Lexie said yes to Echo sleeping over. Maddie couldn't remember a time when Lexie ever said no. Echo used her phone to call and invite the other Scarlet Squad members to the sleepover. Maddie still didn't have any money to get her phone fixed.

They went to the park to kill time, sitting on their favorite swings.

"It's such a nice day," Echo said. "We should have got Dad to load up the ATVs and take us out to the bear trails."

That was something Maddie loved doing with the Blaze family. She was a good driver – confident on the rocky tracks. Echo usually let Maddie drive while she sat on the back.

But she couldn't be bothered today. She didn't want them to be too tired for her plans tonight. Maddie nudged Echo. Plain Face Grace and No Action Jackson were walking through the park right towards them. Grace was wearing a brown gingham church dress.

Maddie smiled sweetly at them. "Got big plans for Thanksgiving?" Grace kept her eyes down on the sidewalk and didn't say a word.

"I meant to say I loved your singing," Maddie continued. "You two are the perfect couple." They kept walking. Maddie could see Jackson holding Grace's arm protectively. Maddie reached in her purse when they'd passed the swings, pulled a tampon out, and tossed it behind Grace.

"Oh, excuse me, Gracie, I think you dropped something!" Maddie called out politely.

Grace looked back and saw the tampon. She went white, bent down, and picked it up, cupping it in her hand as if she were attempting to hide it from Jackson. Then she ran as fast as she could out of sight, holding her Bible in one hand and the tampon in the other. Jackson glared at Maddie and took off after her.

"That's funny ... period!" Maddie yelled as she and Echo burst into laughter.

ELEVEN

Finally, Mom left for her date, and all the Scarlet Squad were in Maddie's family room. It felt good for the house to be full, even if one of those people was Arkadia.

"What kind of pizza does everyone want?" Maddie asked. "Hamburger!" Arkadia suggested.

"Pepperoni," Kaitlyn said.

"Cheese," both Echo and Sophia called out in unison.

Maddie gave the nod. "Then pepperoni and cheese it will be," she announced, looking directly at Arkadia. Then elbowed Echo, who was sitting next to her on the sofa. She didn't want to remind everyone that she was the only one without a phone. Echo picked up on the hint and called to order the pizza.

The girls landed in Maddie's room, pizza boxes in hand. Shadow jumped off the bed and scrambled underneath. "Oh, poor baby," Maddie whispered. "You don't like my friends? Or just Arkadia?"

Kaitlyn picked up Maddie's sketchpad that was

lying on the nightstand. It was open to a page where Maddie had drawn the Scarlet Squad from a photo. "Wow! This is like *really, really* good! Maddie, did you draw this?" She showed the others. "Check it out."

"I want a copy!" Sophia said, inspecting it.

"It's crap," Maddie said. "I stuffed up Echo's nose. I suck at faces." She snatched the sketchpad away and shoved it in a drawer. She divided the pizza up and handed it out with napkins. "Spill and you die," she warned. Her room was spotless, as a rule.

"We have a mission," she announced. "A Scarlet Squad mission. Should you choose to participate and accept the assignment, well, you get to stay in the squad. Otherwise ... good riddance."

The girls listened in closely as Maddie outlined the plan. The pizzas were devoured. Maddie handed out two shopping bags of supplies that she'd already collected from around her house. "Follow me," she said.

The girls did as they were told. They grabbed their coats and headed out the front door, loaded down with the supplies. They trekked through the park, through the suburbs, all the way to the most prestigious gated subdivision in town, Gateway.

"Oh no ... tell me, no," Kaitlyn play protested. "Is our target plain-faced? And a disgrace?" Maddie laughed. "If it smells like a rat, it is indeed a rat," she answered.

Maddie led them to a lovely house on the cul-desac. The lights were all off except for a nightlight in what looked to be a bedroom upstairs.

Maddie divided out the goods. "Echo, you are on egg duty, eggie. And Sophia, you can cream Crisco oil on the car ..."

"The Mercedes?" Sophia panicked. "But ..."

"But what? Yes, the Mercedes!"

Anyone who flaunts their money by buying a Mercedes deserves to have it creamed.

Maddie continued. "Kaitlyn – peanut butter on the white picket fence. Anyone who has a real-life white picket fence is just asking for trouble."

"What about me?" Arkadia asked.

Maddie chuckled and handed her eight rolls of toilet paper. "Go nuts."

"What are you going to do?" Sophia asked.

"I'm the lookout," Maddie answered. "I'm the only one I trust to make sure we don't get caught." The girls got busy. Arkadia was the last to run out of supplies. Maddie took one last look at their creation. The girls had done a great job. Toilet paper was looped all over the trees and bushes. Eggs were smashed all over the front porch, and the car and fence were smeared and looked disgusting.

"Perfect," Maddie said. "Trash deserves to live in a trash bin."

Echo reached into the pocket of her coat and pulled out one last egg. She grinned at Maddie and chucked the egg at the Mercedes.

Suddenly, there was an ear-piercing squeal. The Mercedes flashed and wailed. "Let's go!" Maddie whispered.

The five girls took off, running down the street to the exit, but the gates were closed. Maddie reached for the latch and tried to pull it up. It would not budge. "Cruuud!" she grunted. "Who knew the gates would be locked after 9 pm? Let's climb over."

Maddie, being the tallest, was the first to clear the stone gate. Kaitlyn, being the most athletic, was the second. Sophia got over through sheer determination, and Echo struggled, but after Maddie yelled at her, she finally made it. Arkadia just stood frozen.

"If you don't ... you are out ... I mean, *out* out!" Maddie yelled. The other girls were running towards the park already. Maddie desperately wanted to leave Arkadia behind. But she was afraid Arkadia would be a weakling and give them all up. And surely Maddie would cop the blame. So, she turned back, grabbed Arkadia's arm, and helped pull her over the fence.

Once they were back safe in Maddie's bedroom, the girls resumed their spots on the beds and caught their breath.

"I can't believe what we just did," Sophia admitted. Maddie was beaming. "I know ... we rock ... it was lit!"

Sophia wasn't as amused. "I just mean ... imagine if we were caught. What'd Grace do to piss you off so bad anyway, Mad?"

T. G. Starr

Maddie was getting sick of the way Sophia was standing up to her. She made a disgusted sound. "She was *born*." She grabbed her tablet and gave Echo a pointed look. "Check out what Elmo taught us today."

She went to Grace's profile, right-clicked, and typed in "XXX," just as Elmo had instructed. She was in! She found the screenshot she had saved in the folder marked "Homework." Then copied and pasted the conversation as a post on Grace's page, carefully deleting Kaylie's name as she did:

so if u cld date anyone in the world, who wld it be?

Grace: Jake Taylor.

Maddie logged out then checked Grace's site as a guest. Sure enough, the conversation was plastered on her page for all to see.

Maddie immediately logged into Kaylie's account and posted a message to Grace.

Kaylie: omg, i got hacked. i think u did too

Grace didn't reply. Maddie was sure she was sound asleep. "We'll let it simmer and check back in the morning," Maddie said. "Ready for a round of Sux?"

"Sure," Kaitlyn agreed. "I'll start." The others gathered around.

"Arkadia, your life sucks the most because, well, you're so caught up on Chad, and you don't even know he flirts with Sophia and me."

Arkadia looked like she was about to cry. She took a deep breath and took her turn. "Echo, your life sucks the most because ... you aren't ugly, but you're sure not pretty, and you have bad taste in clothes. You are a real live echo ... you echo whatever Maddie says and always live in her shadow and ..."

"Enough!" Maddie demanded. "Arkadia ..."

"I was already *it*," Arkadia protested.

Maddie continued harshly, "Arkadia. You are pretty much ugly ... you are weak, and we don't really like you ... so your life *really* sucks! Echo, you go ..."

Echo was about to speak when there was a loud crashing noise downstairs. The girls listened closely as another loud crash rang out and then silence.

"What was that?" Kaitlyn cried.

Maddie froze. *Had someone seen them? Followed them home? Was someone breaking in?* But she had a fearless reputation to live up to. So, grabbing an old softball bat out of her closet, she tiptoed down the stairs, her heart pounding out of her chest.

When she reached the bottom of the stairs, she saw her mother desperately trying to stand upright.

"What are *you* doing home?"

Elodie sat her purse and coat on the sofa and fell into the recliner. "Ben got a call ... had to call it a night ... some dang trouble in the gated community ... I mean, they've got a gate for crying out loud."

Maddie's heart began to race even faster than it

had when she thought there was an intruder. She felt nauseated. "Your date was a *cop*?"

"Not any cop ... the new sheriff, darl," Mom slurred.

Maddie started back upstairs to break the news to the girls who were waiting, wide-eyed, to find out what made the noise.

"It's just Mom," Maddie informed them as she sat back on her bed, smoothing the comforter. The girls sighed in relief. "I thought she was out for the night," Sophia said. "Too high maintenance for her date or what?"

"Probably," Maddie laughed. "But ... well ... her date got called in to check out a disturbance at Gateway. It turns out he's the new sheriff."

Complete silence filled the room.

"I'm all done," Kaitlyn said. "My parents would kill me if they found out."

"Concur," Sophia chimed in. "If we slide by this one, I promise to God I'll never do anything that dumb again. Besides, I keep hearing Grace singing "Amazing Grace" in my head, and it's freakin' me out."

The other girls agreed ... all except Maddie.

TWELVE

It was well after midnight when the girls finally fell asleep. They didn't wake up until after 10 am the following day when the neighbor decided to jackhammer his back porch.

"It should be illegal to make all that noise this early," Echo complained as she hid her head under her pillow.

"Don't even say that word ... *illegal*," Sophie said.

It was a rocky start to the day, so Maddie decided it was time for breakfast. "Pretty sure there's some cereal stashed," she told them. "And be quiet ... Mom's off today."

The girls sat at the round kitchen table. Maddie went to grab a box of cereal, but there wasn't any.

Crap! Guess that's what happens when you have cereal for dinner every night.

"How about toast?" Maddie asked, setting a stack of plates out onto the countertop.

Before the girls could dive in, there was a knock at the door.

It was the sheriff. He was a short, stocky man with

shifty brown eyes and dark hair balding badly on top. He wore a blue uniform and a shiny silver badge.

Maddie managed a shaky "Good morning."

"You must be Maddison," the sheriff drawled with a thick Texan accent. "I'm Ben Kirby. Is your mother around?"

"I am!"

Maddie jumped. She hadn't heard her mom come up behind her.

"Come on in, Ben. You'll have to excuse me. I'm a hot mess ... just waking up."

They all walked into the kitchen. Elodie noticed the girls at the kitchen table. "There's no way in Hades you girls are eating toast for breakfast. Your parents would think I was a horrible mother."

Yeah ... and the man you're trying to impress. I hate how you pretend to be such a good mother for the sake of your reputation when you can't even buy enough cereal to last the week. Always plenty of vodka, though.

Mom motioned the sheriff to the table and pulled up a barstool chair. "Maddie, you sit on the barstool, and Ben, you can have a seat right here ..." She pointed to the chair where Maddie had previously sat. "I'll whip us up some *real* breakfast. Now, what brings us the honor of your company, Ben?"

The sheriff took a seat and removed his cap.

"Fresh coffee?" Elodie asked, tightening the sash on her purple velvet housecoat.

He nodded. "Yes, ma'am." Then he smiled a

mouthful of yellow teeth at the girls. "I'm Sheriff Ben. Pleased to meet y'all. I wanted to apologize to the lovely Elodie for having to bolt out last night," he said. "I've only been in Pine Cove a minute, but when I took the job, I was told things are relatively quiet around here. But I guess that doesn't go for juvenile delinquents. Darn kids did a number over at the Harwood place, I reckon."

The girls grew silent.

Sheriff Kirby glanced around the table. All eyes were on him. "Those hoodlums did hundreds of dollars of damage. They tried to ruin the paint job on their brand spanking new Mercedes, not to mention the Harwoods have to hire a landscaper to remove all the toilet paper from their trees. A right nice God-fearin' family too, doctor, lawyer, and two nice kids."

Mom furiously shook her head. "Bet some time in the slammer would do the brats some good." She opened the refrigerator. "Where's the eggs? I *just* bought two cartons of eggs! Now, where in tarnation are they?"

Maddie felt the blood run from her head to her toes. "How about we have ... uh ..." Maddie started. She was desperately trying to think of something that didn't require eggs. "Oatmeal! You make the best oatmeal, Mom."

"Oatmeal it will be ... you do like oats, don't you, Ben?" Maddie couldn't recall her mother *ever* making oatmeal. Still, Elodie was a sucker for a compliment, so she got a big carton of oatmeal from the cupboard, still perplexed about the eggs.

The sheriff said that he did, indeed, like oatmeal. "Long as ya got some peanut butter to go in it."

The girls' eyes grew as round as saucers.

"We always have peanut butter," Elodie said as she scrambled around the pantry in search of the jar of peanut butter. "Well ... looks like we're all out. I'm so sorry."

Mom whipped up a big bowl of lumpy oatmeal and dished it out. The girls wolfed theirs down and excused themselves from the table.

Elodie called Maddie back to the table. "Ben wanted to talk to you about something," she said, pointing for Maddie to sit back down on the barstool.

Maddie sat down. She could hardly breathe. She hoped he couldn't see her heart beating through her chest or that her body was shaking.

"I asked your mamma to lunch today at the Big Bear," he explained. "I would be honored if you would join us."

Maddie didn't want to go. His Texas accent bugged her, for one thing. Also, she had no desire to be around a cop, especially after the stunts she'd pulled lately. But she was so relieved that going to lunch was all he wanted to talk to her about, she accepted without hesitation.

"Sure!" she answered. "Mom, can I go upstairs with the girls now?"

Elodie dismissed her daughter. Maddie ran upstairs. She was shaken but hopeful that she had skirted by yet another near disaster.

"That was close," Sophia sighed. "Too much drama for me!"

"And me!" Kaitlyn said.

Maddie got her tablet out. "Well, we're safe in cyberspace," she said. "Let's see what Dis Grace has to say about the Jake post." She logged in and clicked on Grace's page. The post was still there.

Beneath the post, Grace had commented. "I was hacked, and I don't know how to get this off." Someone was typing below Grace's comment.

"Oh ... my ... god!" Maddie wailed. "It's Chloe about to comment ... this is going to get good."

"Jake is mine," Chloe's comment read. "Back off!"

The girls gathered around, watching the drama unfold, laughing.

*

Elodie and Maddie met Ben at the Big Bear, a quaint and cozy diner on Main Street. It was the most popular place to eat in town, the go-to family spot, and hang out for teens. The three sat at a table, and Elodie ordered a vodka tonic.

"Aren't you having a beer?" she asked the sheriff.

He shook his head. "No, I'm technically on duty ... or will be after lunch. Gotta go back over to the Harwoods'. I'm determined to get to the bottom of this bad behavior. It will simply not be tolerated, come hell or high water. There's a new sheriff in town!" He let out a big roar of laughter.

Mom reached into her purse and pulled out a jumbo-sized lipstick. She reapplied another red layer and batted her thickly painted eyes. "We sure appreciate your service," she said. "The last sheriff wouldn't even give out a speeding ticket."

Or a DUI or a DWI. He preferred to take that favor out in trade, I bet.

"So, I hear," Sheriff Kirby replied. "Makes no sense at all to me. I come from Texas, you know. Don't mess with Texas! I intend to bring that same message to Pine Cove."

Maddie was quickly losing her appetite, but she didn't get to eat out often. She ordered a cheeseburger and then tuned out the adults' conversation.

"You seem like a right nice young lady, Maddison," Ben was saying when she realized he was talking to her. "I would love for you to help Miss Peterson get the group started and on track."

Maddie had no idea what he was talking about.

"A right *rude* young lady," Elodie scolded. "In case you weren't listening, Ben's been telling us how he's going to bring changes to the community. He's talking to the new therapist later today about starting a high school group. He said Mr. Freeman mentioned at the Town Council meeting that some shady shenanigans are going on lately. I told him I'm sure he can count on you ... right, honey?"

Conveniently, the waitress arrived with their food.

Maddie looked around the room to avoid eye contact with the sheriff. That's when she saw them in lovers' corner. Jake and Chloe were in the secluded booth reserved for couples.

Jake was feeding Chloe a bite off his plate, and she was laughing. Maddie could see their legs twisted together underneath the table. She wanted to cry.

Chloe pointed to Maddie and shot her signature Miss America wave. Jake looked at her with his green, green eyes, then immediately turned away as if he was disgusted by the sight of her. Maddie turned back to her mother and Ben. She hoped they hadn't noticed how she was belittled. She hoped no one noticed. The last thing she needed was to be humiliated in public. If there was any humiliating to be done, she was the one who was going to do it.

THIRTEEN

M addie signed in as Kaylie that night.

Kaylie: u on, chica?

Grace: Yes.

Kaylie: what's up with that Jake drama on your page?

Grace: I didn't post that. You were right. I got hacked too. I can't get it off my wall.

Kaylie: hayden's rele bummed

Grace: Will you tell him I didn't post that?

Kaylie: u do the explaining, eggie. but ive got ur back

Grace: Thank you, eggie.

Maddie stopped for a minute to laugh, then switched profiles.

Hayden: Gracie, are you there?

Grace: Yes.

Hayden: Kaylie told me you want to chat.

Grace: Yes. I wanted to tell you I didn't post that about

Jake. I don't even know him, really. But unfortunately, I got hacked, and it won't delete.

Hayden: I was sweatin' it. We still on for Telluride?

Grace: If my parents allow it, we are.

Hayden: We are going to be there earlier than I thought. How does Christmas Eve Eve sound?

Grace: Didn't know there was such a thing. LOL.

Hayden: December 23rd. I'll catch up to you later with all the details.

Maddie's bedroom door was slung wide open. "Hurry, grab your coat, and get in the car!" Elodie shouted frantically. She ran back down the stairs.

Maddie closed the chat with Hayden, grabbed her coat, purse and tablet, and ran down to the car.

Her mother took off, tires spinning.

"Why didn't you answer your phone?" Elodie was screaming.

"I don't have a phone," Maddie reminded her. "Geez, don't you remember ... you broke it?"

"Don't you remember, you were in a whole bunch of trouble?" Elodie had clearly been drinking, running stop signs, and speeding through red lights.

Maddie was afraid for her life. "Mom, slow down! Where are we going?"

"The hospital! Your sister ... Samuel beat her up. Her neighbor called and was taking her and Liam to the hospital."

"Liam? Is he hurt too?" Maddie was shaking.

"He's fine, but we need you to hold him while I'm with Ashley," Elodie said. "Ben's meeting us there. God help that ... that ... sorry excuse for a man, that Samuel ... he's in for it now ... no more deadbeat cops in our town."

Elodie flew into the hospital parking lot, parked in a tow-away zone, and ran inside. Maddie was right behind her. They were met at the entrance by Ashley's elderly neighbor, who handed the baby and his diaper bag over to Maddie. Maddie held Baby Liam close and found a bottle for him in the diaper bag while Mom went to be with Ash. She sat on the couch in the waiting room and fed him until he fell fast asleep.

Mom appeared. "How's Ash?"

"She's busted up pretty good. He broke her arm and bruised her face. She's getting stitches on her forehead, and she's upset and scared. But, other than that, she's fine."

Maddie looked at the baby, sleeping peacefully in her arms. She wished she could change the world for him.

Mom went back to Ash, and soon after, the sheriff arrived in full uniform. "Hello, Maddison," he said. "I'm so sorry about your sister."

"Thank you. Mom's with her now, down the corridor in the emergency room."

"Boy, this town is one lively place," he said in his long Texan accent. "The Harwood case escalated with some cyber activity, and one thing led to another 'til I'd practically spent the whole dadgum afternoon there ... and now this. But rest assured, I'll have that hoodlum creep Samuel behind bars." He tore off down the hall.

Maddie took a deep breath.

Escalated? Wonder what that means.

The baby began to stir, so she walked around, cradling him in her arms, looking out of the windows at the people passing by. She was caught totally off guard. It was Jake right outside in the courtyard. Jake and ... Grace! They were hugging. Maddie's heart was racing. Her hands were shaking. The baby was crying, but she couldn't resist. Gently placing Liam on the sofa, she grabbed her tablet and ran to the glass window, where she snapped a photo. *Ha. Caught in the act.*

She went back to the couch and tried to console Liam. He continued to scream until she finally got him to take his bottle. She clicked onto TeenScene and went straight to Grace's site. "XXX," she typed.

Within seconds the profile picture on Grace's page was changed. *Now she's going to pay.*

FOURTEEN

It was Thanksgiving Day. Maddie wore a teal-blue sweater and dangly turkey earrings Echo had given her. She couldn't help but notice how the sweater brought out the blue in her eyes.

"How do ya like me now?" she asked her reflection in the mirror, pretending it was Jake.

Maybe if I had even bluer eyes ... or bigger boobs, would he like me then?

"You are moving back here for good, right?" Maddie asked Ashley as they sat at the kitchen bar. Maddie was meticulously peeling potatoes while Ashley held the baby with her one good arm. Her other arm was in a cast.

Ashley and Liam had stayed at home with Mom and Maddie since Ash was released from the hospital. She was too terrified to go back where Samuel could show up at any time.

"I don't know, Mad. Mom's so much to deal with."

Maddie stopped peeling. "Mom is so much to deal with? What about Samuel? I hope you're not thinking of going back to him."

"Of course not!"

"Happy Thanksgiving." Grandma Betty called out as she walked into the kitchen. She had an armload of pies and sat them on the counter. "Pecan, chocolate, lemon, and pumpkin ... whatever your fancy, you'll find it here." She produced a cooler bag and set it down as well. "And cookies for my girls and the little prince."

Maddie hugged her. "You're the best, Gran," she told her. And she was. Grandma Betty always took up the slack in the areas her mother fell short. She was loving. She was understanding. She was giving. And she baked!

"That is so sweet, but you know Liam can't have cookies yet, Grandma?" Ashley said. "Give that poor baby some cookies. They're not going to hurt him. Shoot, your mother was raised on…"

The girls and Grandma realized what she was saying and broke into laughter.

"Let me hold that little prince! Poor baby, already seeing how cruel the world can be." Maddie couldn't agree more. Ashley handed Liam to Grandma Betty, wincing as she moved her broken arm.

"And as for the devil that did that to you ... I've got something for him!" Grandma raged, doubling her fist. "Your momma wouldn't listen to me about anything, thought she knew it all. Your father was nothing but a lying cheat, but oh no, Elodie knew better ... until she didn't, that is. By golly, you will not make the same mistakes."

Maddie put the peeled and cubed potatoes in a pot of boiling water.

The doorbell rang: it was Uncle Robert and Aunt Gina with their kids, four-year-old Awful Aiden and three-year-old Tera the Terrible. Before she could dodge, Aunt Gina was kissing Maddie on the cheek. If anyone wore as much makeup as her mother did, it was her aunt. *Must run in the family.* Ashley laughed under her breath, so Maddie knew she was sporting a giant red lip print on her cheek.

Robert was right behind her, reeking of stale cigar smoke. "Hello, pretty ladies!" He always greeted the sisters the same way.

"This must be the new royal addition to the family. What a handsome little man," Aunt Gina said, tickling Liam's tiny feet. "Kids, come and meet your baby cousin."

The children blasted into the kitchen. Ashley held the baby tighter as the kids got obnoxiously close. Tera tried to poke his eye, but Ashley gently moved her hand. Then she grabbed Liam's bottle.

"Mine!" her brother argued.

Maddie took the bottle from Tera, and both kids began to scream at the top of their lungs. Poor Liam. He was so innocent. He hadn't done anything to deserve these brats messing with him.

For a split second, Grace's baby picture flashed

through her mind. But Maddie quickly dismissed feeling sorry for her. Grace had it all – a family who loved her, parents who earned great money, and a not-boyfriend who was always there for her.

And she can sing. I wish I could sing.

The sheriff arrived, was introduced around, and everyone finally sat down to eat.

"Good food. Good peeps. Good gosh, let's eat!" Sheriff Kirby announced, initiating a toast with his tea. "Y'all are too kind to invite me."

"Maddie, you are turning into quite the young lady," Aunt Gina said. "I mean, look at those long legs, and you're even getting a little figure."

Yeah, quite the young lady ... not quite the beautiful young lady. Long and tall ... and kind of flat.

Maddie thanked her aunt politely. She knew better than not to. "What do you want to be when you grow up?" Aunt Gina asked.

The question took Maddie by surprise. She hadn't spent much time thinking about it. "Ummm ... I dunno. Maybe a photographer."

Yeah, photography for sure. I'm an excellent picture taker!

She couldn't wait to check Grace's page with the new picture on it. With Ashley and the baby there and it being Thanksgiving, she hadn't been able to log on at all.

"You should see her drawings," Grandma Betty said with pride. "She's very talented."

"I'm sure you'll make an excellent photographer or artist, Maddie," Aunt Gina replied. "You're such a perfectionist."

Perfectionist ... why sugar-coat it? Yeah ... I'm OCD. Go ahead and say it.

"Ashley, I will need to get a formal statement from you after dinner," Sheriff Kirby announced inappropriately. "I hate to bother you with all that, but I think you'll be pleased to know that ole Sammer is now in the slammer."

There was complete silence. Aunt Gina and Uncle Robert shared a puzzled glance.

"Yup ... he won't be pickin' on you again ... it's just not going to happen. Not on *my* watch," Ben concluded.

"I, for one, am delighted to hear the news," Grandma Betty rejoiced. "Hopefully, he never sees the light of day again."

"We're turning a new leaf here in Pine Cove," promised Ben. "Prosecuting to the fullest. We'll teach 'em the joy of bustin' rocks around here. We're vamping up preventative resources too. So, Maddie, that reminds me ... got somethin' to talk to you about too."

Maddie tried not to look as nervous as she was.

"Oh?" she asked. *I'm busy for the rest of my life. I have no time to talk to you.*

The sheriff shook his head. "I've been talking to Mr. Freeman ..."

Maddie was on the spot. She felt like she was going to puke up the mouthful of potatoes she had just swallowed. What could she say? "OK," she managed.

"Sounds like you're takin' care of biz," Robert said. "Glad to have you overseein' this town."

"You don't even know the half of it," Ben went on since he had a captive audience. "The kids in this town are out of control. There's this new site on the computer for teens, called TeenSpace, TeenFace ... no, TeenScene. Since it's brand new, there's no real security. It's kind of intentional because that's how the platform lures kids to it ... they can create fake accounts and do whatever they want. Unlike the other sites, this one doesn't seem to be monitored at all. Well, when I was over yonder at the Harwoods', the little boy, Gavin, told me about his sister getting bullied on TeenScene. I took a look, and sure 'nuff, he was right. This sleepy little town is about to have the biggest wake-up call they've ever had."

Maddie couldn't eat another bite. She faked a headache and went upstairs.

She pulled out her tablet. Finally, she could see what the photo had stirred up, but Ashley burst into the room before she could read them. There were fifty-three comments on the picture. Lots of people had tagged Chloe so that she would see it. Some comments were calling Grace rude names and others with vaguely menacing emojis like skulls and coffins.

111

Grace had written a comment: I don't know who took the picture. I don't know who posted it. I was hugging Jake because his grandfather had just died.

"What do you think you're doing?" she asked. "I know you don't have a headache."

"I do now."

Ashley peered over Maddie's shoulders. "Who's Kaylie? What are you up to, Mad?" Maddie pulled the tablet back and turned it off. "At my age, you were running around smoking and drinking and ... well ... lots of bad things. You have a baby and aren't married. Your baby's daddy just beat the hell out of you and is now in jail. And you're worried because I'm online? Serious?"

"Yeah ... I did all that. But don't forget who was here for you when Mom wasn't," Ashley said with tears streaming down her cheeks. "I love you and just want the best for you."

Maddie knew it was true.

"Don't cry. You'll ruin your mascara."

Ashley wiped her tears. "Look, Sophia stopped by the other day. She's worried about you. I am too."

"She should be worried about herself," Maddie spat. *How dare Sophia stick her nose into my life.*

Ash sighed. "I don't know what you're into or what you are doing in the shadows, but somebody's going to get hurt."

Maddie knew what her sister was saying was right. Ashley always was. One day Maddie would tell her all about it. About Jake and Chloe. About Grace and how she couldn't stand her face. She'd tell her lots of things. But not now. She was on a mission. She had a personal vendetta with the world, and she couldn't stop even if she wanted.

FIFTEEN

Thanksgiving break was over. Back to school. Maddie met up with Echo in the park when she saw a flash of red as Jake's car whizzed past.

Crap, he must have fixed the paint job already. I thought he wouldn't be able to pick up Chloe in the car for at least a few more days.

Maddie had committed not to tell the Scarlet Squad about the Grace and Jake photo. She knew the minute they saw it, they'd know she did it, but why confess? The Squad was changing. Sophia had broken trust when she spilled it with Ashley. Kaitlyn always sided with Sophia, so she couldn't be fully counted on. Arkadia was barely hanging on to her status because of Chad. But, after seeing Jake's car, Maddie decided that there would be no harm in telling Echo. She needed to get it off her chest.

"Been on TeenScene lately?" Maddie began as the two hit the sidewalk and picked up the pace towards school. The wind was cold, and once again, Maddie was a little too scantily dressed for the frigid weather.

"Nope, had a house full of company, and Elmo is

snoopin' me," Echo answered. "He doesn't want me on TeenScene. He's *such* a big brother."

Maddie shuddered to think of what he'd do if he knew what she was into online. "Well, Samuel beat Ashley up, and we were at the hospital with her," Maddie stated.

Echo stopped in her tracks. "How is she? Is he in jail?"

"She'll be all right, and yes, he's in jail, and I hope they throw away the key," Maddie hurried. "But the big drama is Grace. She was hugging Jake at the hospital."

The girls cut across the parking lot.

Echo gasped. "Oh my God! That's crazy."

"I guess his grandpa died."

"Oh ... that's sad. But what's up with Grace and him?"

"I got the best snap ever of the big hug," Maddie said. "I posted it as Grace's profile. And ... get this ... when a hack post goes on ... it won't come off."

Echo was cracking up. "Oh my god, girl. That's sick! You are mean ... like, savage mean."

"If you tell anyone, even a Scarlet, you will pay ... I promise," Maddie warned.

Echo held out her pinky. It had been a solemn tradition to pinky swear since they were little girls. "I swear ... I pinky promise swear," she declared. Maddie linked pinkies, and the deal was sealed.

The girls reached the school grounds and dashed

inside to warm up. They hurried to math and took their assigned seats. As usual, Maddie was right behind Grace. It was apparent from the stares and whispers directed towards Grace that their classmates had seen the picture.

Isabella leaned over and whispered to Grace, "I can't believe you did that. Chloe's really salty."

Grace looked as if she was going to cry.

Mrs. Motts stood before the class. "Before we get started, Maddie, may I see you for a moment?"

Maddie was caught totally off guard. What could Motts want now? She hadn't even said a word to Grace today. Maddie felt nervous but tried not to show it.

"Mr. Freeman would like to speak to you after class."

"OK," Maddie agreed as if she had a choice.

Run! Run as fast as you can. Hide! Leave school and maybe even the country. Now!

*

Despite protests from her inner voice, Maddie landed in Mr. Freeman's office immediately after class. He looked as serious as ever except for the snowmen all over his festive new tie. "Thank you for coming," he said as he met her at his secretary's desk and walked her back to his office.

Maddie's heart felt as if it would pound out of her chest. She could hardly breathe. What had she done now?

"I am not as dumb as you think I am," Freeman was saying, his dark eyes fixated on her. "Trust me. I am aware of ... a myriad of situations. I am offering you a chance at redemption. You see, in the state of Colorado, public schools are held responsible for students' behavior when it comes to delinquency. To be in a position of authority and to knowingly *not* report bad behavior such as bullying is ... well, it is illegal. You may or may not be aware, but there is a new sheriff in town – Ben Kirby."

Mr. Freeman stopped talking to give Maddie a chance to acknowledge or deny that she knew him. She did neither.

"Sheriff Ben and I spent a good amount of time discussing the subject over the vacation," Mr. Freeman continued. "Together, we have come up with several solutions to some severe problems. Here's where you come in. We are starting a therapy class for behavioral issues, namely, bullying. Since you are a student who is one of the main antagonists here at Pine Cove High, we have unanimously agreed that you will be the group's first member. The leader, in fact."

This is not happening.

"It's not optional," he continued. "If you are to remain in this school, you *will* be required to be a member of the group, and you *will* work with the new counselor, Miss Nancy Peterson, who has joined us here at Pine Cove High. I think you will find her quite pleasant and helpful." Maddie was freaking out. Her life was over. Her reputation was soon to be in tatters. Leading a group against bullies? What would everyone think? What would become of the Scarlet Squad?

"I have arranged for you to be excused from the rest of your classes today so you and Miss Peterson can get acquainted," Freeman said. "That's how imperative your full cooperation in this group is, Maddison. We are counting on you, and I suggest you take full advantage of the resources that will be at your disposal. Otherwise, you are in for a very rude awakening."

Mr. Freeman led Maddie down the carpeted hallway that connected his office with the vice principal's office, counselor's office, and teachers' lounge. He took a left at the counselor's office, where a young woman was busy unpacking boxes.

She looked at Maddie and offered a kind smile. She was slim and short and looked to be in her mid-twenties. Her eyes were a warm shade of hazel that perfectly matched her shoulder-length shiny hair. Maddie couldn't help but feel drawn in but stopped short when she caught herself.

This is a set-up. Don't give anything away.

"I'll leave you two chicks to chat," Mr. Freeman said as he left the room. "Did he call us *chicks?*" the counselor laughed.

Maddie smirked. "Pretty sure he did."

We're not on the same team, woman.

"Maddie, please call me Nancy," the counselor said. "Take a seat. I'm obviously new here. I could use your help unpacking and learning a bit about the school situation. I gather you're quite popular." She put a box of jumbled stationery on the desk.

"I'm not in the popular group," Maddie said. *You don't know anything about me.*

"You know, Maddie, I was a lot like you when I was in school," Nancy said. "Just a teen girl trying to get by, doin' what it took to come out of those years in one piece. I made some bad choices, though, and ended up in so much trouble you would never believe. But I wouldn't change all that. It made me who I am today."

Oh, vomit. Bet you've never faced anything tough. This is all just a script.

Maddie fiddled with a little container of thumbtacks. It felt good to press the sharp point into her finger pad.

"I was an angry teenager," Nancy's face was earnest. "I think you might feel the same way. Mr. Freeman told me about your family situation. I can see how it might make you want to be in control at school."

Maddie was surprised to feel her throat choke up. She gritted her teeth. *Don't you dare cry in front of her.*

"I can relate to abandonment issues," Nancy continued quietly. "I mean, to feel like being left was your fault and feeling different, maybe unlovable. You see, I was adopted. I was told my mother was young,

119

and her mother talked her into giving me up for adoption. A Hispanic family adopted me – Mom, Dad, and two older brothers. They were wonderful, but the problem was ... I am clearly not Hispanic. Our relatives and friends were all Hispanic. We went to a Hispanic church, and I attended a predominantly Hispanic school. I was a misfit if there ever was one. I was so hellbent on feeling like I was unwanted by my *real* parents that I barely saw how wanted I was by the family who adopted me."

Nancy continued. "I turned mean as hell. I learned to fight, and that led me to a world of trouble." She pouted her lips and made a silly face. "Seriously. I can't count how many times I went to juvie ... and later, to the real slammer."

Maddie was shocked. "You went to prison?"

"I spent months waiting in jail, and when I was convicted and got my sentence, I waited two more months in jail until I was transferred to a prison where I did my time" Nancy paused. "It all worked out, though. While I was in the Big House, I got a chance to join a group called Kind Heart Club. And now, you get that opportunity too. Only you don't have to go to prison. Instead, you get to do it here at school."

Kind Heart Club ... that's the lamest thing I've ever heard.

Maddie opened another box. Her eyes grew wide. Inside were at least a dozen cell phones, brand new, all neatly packaged within. All gold in color.

"Oh, just put that box to the side, if you will," Nancy said. "Those will come into play later when the group is established. I want all the KH members to have access to a phone. That way, when they run into trouble and need support, it's there."

"When will the group be formed?" Maddie asked. She didn't really care. In fact, she dreaded it entirely. But she did need a phone. And the gold phone looked amazing.

"I figure by the first of the year when we come back from winter break," Nancy answered. Maddie nodded. The first of the year was way too long to wait for a phone. She needed one now. Her tablet was great for some stuff, but you can't just fit it in your pocket and make calls that easily. Plus, she had other plans for it. And those plans were right around the corner ... on Christmas Eve Eve.

Nancy went to the restroom. Finally, the moment had come where she was alone. Maddie checked the hallway. The coast was clear. Carefully, she took a phone from the box and slid it into her purse.

*

Maddie rushed home after school. She figured she could handle Nancy – all she had to do was pretend to be nice for a while. Put on a happy face. Pretend she could change.

She grabbed her tablet and logged into TeenScene as Hayden. She was a bit worried about the "myriad of situations" Mr. Freeman was hinting at. She wanted to set up her plan, just in case.

Hayden: Gracie ...?

Grace: Yes. How funny. My parents and my little brother call me Gracie.

Hayden: No one at school calls you Gracie?

Grace: No. Some of the mean girls call me other things, though.

Hayden: Oh? Like what?

Grace: Like Plain Face Grace or Dis Grace.

Omg ... How hilarious! I guess she pays more attention than I thought.

Hayden: No beach. I can have them tended to ... if you want. I know people.

Grace: Oh, no. I would never do that. I believe that kindness prevails, no matter what. You know ... smile, and the world smiles back at you. Besides, I always ask myself, "What would Jesus do?"

Are you ... serious?

Hayden: You're such an eggie. You are practically perfect, a good Christian girl, intelligent and cute. I'm so lucky.

Grace: I'm not perfect, that's for sure. I sin like everyone else.

Hayden: Yeah, right, eggie. Tell me something wrong you did today.

Grace: OK. But you can't tell anyone.

Oh, this is going to be good.

Hayden: Swear!

Grace: I've been keeping something from my parents and everyone else.

Hayden: What? I won't tell.

Grace: I've been passing out. I did it again today. No one saw me. I was in the girl's bathroom.

Hayden: Why don't you tell your parents?

Grace: My mother's a doctor and a worrywart. I don't want to upset her.

Hayden: You should tell her.

Grace: Well, there's another reason too.

Hayden: What's that?

Grace: She'll want to prick my finger for a blood test. That makes me faint.

Hayden: You're fainting anyway.

Grace: Yeah. I know, and I know it's wrong to keep anything from my parents.

Hayden: What do you think is wrong with you?

Grace: I think I have diabetes.

Hayden: Then why not get checked?

Grace: Because then I'll have to have blood tests, and I

faint when I see blood.

Hayden: Can we make plans for Xmas Eve Eve

Grace: Yes!

Hayden: December 23rd. 7 pm sharp. The Birdhouse in Ophir.

Grace: I love that place!

Hayden: I stayed out in my new car later than I was supposed to and might be grounded from electronics. So, if you don't hear from me before then, it's only because I'm grounded. That OK?

Grace: Yes!

Hayden: I'm going to make reservations. Can't wait to meet you.

Grace: See you at The Birdhouse.

Maddie was laughing so hard she feared her ribs were breaking. She was way too good at this. But then she remembered her predicament. She took a deep breath and deleted first Hayden's, then Kaylie's profiles. Then she deleted the whole TeenScene app and all her saved photos and screenshots in the "Homework" file. There was nothing left on the tablet except school apps.

She felt empty and lonely. Almost as if she'd lost a friend.

SIXTEEN

Maddie had no idea what to wear to court. She'd forgotten about Samuel's trial, with everything else on her mind. But she'd promised Ash she'd hold Liam and take him outside if he started to cry – neither of them could trust their mom.

The Honorable Judge Wilson called the court to order. Maddie felt Ash stiffen beside her when she saw him. Although a jury had been selected, Samuel had accepted a deal offered by the prosecution at his attorney's advice. He had pleaded guilty to aggravated assault and was sentenced to six years in prison.

Sheriff Kirby made his debut in the courtroom. Samuel was then led in by the bailiff, wild-eyed and scraggly. He was handcuffed and in shackles.

"He looks like a mad man!" Maddie told Ashley in a low voice as she hugged Liam closer to her.

The judge had a private talk with Samuel and had him swear in and sign the paperwork. Maddie couldn't stand the sight of him, so she took the opportunity to take Liam out to the lobby. "You all right?" Maddie asked when the court was dismissed, and Ashley met her out in the hallway.

"Fine!" Ashley said. "Let's get the hell out of here. Thanks for watching the baby."

"Good riddance to him. He got what he deserved," Elodie mused.

Sheriff Kirby appeared. "Told ya I'm gonna rid this town of all the bad guys," he bragged. "Lodie, wanna go get a bite to eat? Puttin' away criminals makes me very hungry."

"How could I turn down such a lovely offer from such a handsome gentleman?"

"See you later, girls."

Maddie rode with Ashley in her beat-up 1980 Volkswagen. Usually, she'd be embarrassed to ride in the old car she referred to as "The Bomb," but today, she didn't care. They were going to Ashley's apartment to pack up her things, she and the baby were moving back home for good, and Maddie couldn't be happier.

"I freaked out when I saw the judge – did you recognize him?" Ash asked. Maddie tried to remember his face, but she had only glanced at him.

"Do you remember playing in the woods?" Ash prompted. "At the old house. And we found that treehouse."

Maddie remembered. Ash had been so angry at her Mom and Dad. Maddie had been too young to understand why, but they'd destroyed a treehouse they'd found, and it seemed to make Ash feel better.

"That was his. William Wilson. Remember? Willie? He was like a nerdy teenager ten years older than me. And now he's a judge." Ash shuddered. "We're so lucky kids grow up. If he held a grudge, I'd be screwed. He could have let Samuel out on probation or something."

For a moment, Maddie wondered what Grace might become when she grew up. And Jackson. And, oh, any of those nobodies who'd crossed her. She felt a little sick.

*

Maddie called Echo on the new gold phone when they were back home later that night.

Echo answered on the second ring.

She's so desperate. At least I wait for three, sometimes four.

"Hey! Sup?" Maddie said.

Echo was quiet for a moment. Then, "Mad, is that you?"

"Well, yeah ... who else would it be?"

"It's coming up with a weird number," Echo said.

"Oh, just ignore that ... it's a loaner," Maddie fibbed. "So, how did you *beep beep* do without me at school today? Any *beep beep* drama?"

"Mad, you cut out," Echo complained.

"I asked how you *beep beep* did without me in school today."

127

Maddie was growing frustrated. Every time the phone beeped, the screen flashed yellow. "I'll just see you tomorrow."

"Be sure to wear red."

"OK!"

Maddie wanted to throw the phone across the room. What was wrong with the stupid thing anyway? Kind Heart Club – what a sham.

SEVENTEEN

I t seemed to Maddie like she had waited forever for this day – December 23rd, the eve of Christmas Eve. She woke up the minute the sun came streaming in her bedroom window. Down the hallway, she could hear little Liam fussing for his breakfast. It was nice to have them home, close to her.

"I'll give him his bottle, get some rest," she told her sister, poking her head into the spare room. "OK," Ashley agreed. "Aren't we in a generous mood? But I'm not gonna turn ya down. I'm not crazy."

Maddie kissed her nephew on the cheek and took him downstairs. Then, heating his bottle, she waltzed around the kitchen, making him smile.

Mom was in a rush to get to work.

"People are crawlin' out of the woodwork to get their shopping done," she grumbled, slapping on another layer of purple lipstick. "Thank God we're closed after tonight, which reminds me, Ben and I are going out after work, and then he will be joining us for Christmas dinner. Will you tidy up the house?"

"Sure," Maddie answered, a little more chipper than she meant to be. She didn't want it to be too obvious how happy she was.

Cleaning the house was a good distraction for the day. The floors and surfaces sparkled. The baby clothes were washed, dried, and folded. Maddie admired her work. But without access to TeenScene, she was worried something would go wrong with the plan. She wished she could watch it all go down, but that would be impossible since it was in Ophir.

I should hide down the street from Grace's and make sure they go. She better not chicken out on her hot date.

"Goin' out?" Ashley asked as Maddie came downstairs. "Yeah, just going for a walk ... maybe to Echo's." Ashley held the baby out for his auntie to kiss.

"See ya later, big boy," Maddie told him.

"Make good choices!" Ashley kidded. She knew how Maddie hated being told that.

Maddie pictured Grace's face when she discovered Hayden stood her up. What a first date. *I can't believe she had the nerve to think Jake was cute. Or the nerve to believe a hot guy like Hayden would be into her. This'll teach her.*

She walked to Gateway. The gates were locked. *Security must have been tightened due to the incident. The gates weren't usually closed at this time.*

Like the universe meant for it to happen, a truck pulled up and punched in the code at the perfect moment for her to enter.

It was dusk. Maddie hurried up Grace's street, sticking by the tree line. When she reached the house, her heart began to race.

"Go poo-poo potty?" she heard a girl's voice ask as the front door opened. It was Grace.

No. Don't let it be a dog.

Sure enough, Grace's Basset Hound burst through the doorway. Maddie remembered seeing pictures of Baxter on TeenScene. She made herself as small as possible behind a tree and some bushes. The stupid dog came straight towards her. She was screwed.

"Baxter ... hurry up and do your business," Grace called.

The dog continued to rush through the bushes towards Maddie. She shut her eyes and held her breath. Then, she felt a warm wetness on her leg.

No ... no ... yuck! It pissed on me!

"I've got a treat for you," Grace coaxed. Baxter chose the treat over any further sniffing. He barreled back through the bushes, took the awaiting treat, and went inside the house.

Maddie was recovering from the close encounter with Baxter when the door opened again. "Come on, kids," Grace's father was saying.

The family trooped towards the car. "You look lovely, Grace," Grace's mom said. "Just remember, though, be yourself."

Maddie tried not to snort. Grace was wearing a calf-length plain blue dress with matching blue tights. She looked frumpy, like a thirty-year-old.

What was she thinking? Does she not have any idea about fashion at all?

The car backed out of the driveway and down the street.

Maddie started sneaking home. Her wet jeans stunk. By the time she got near the school, it was almost 7 pm. She had to make her phone call to The Birdhouse soon. If she waited much longer, the Harwoods might catch onto the fact Hayden wasn't going to show. They could leave the restaurant at any moment. She had programmed the number for the restaurant into her phone earlier. She pressed 'call.' Her heart raced with every ring.

"It's a wonderful day at The Birdhouse. How may I help you?"

Maddie cleared her dry throat. "I need to page someone, please," she managed, her voice hoarse.

"Sure, no problem," the girl said.

Maddie tried to say the name, but her phone was beeping and flashing red. "Pardon? You seem to be cutting out," the girl told her.

Maddie repeated herself. The phone was going crazy. Maddie couldn't hear herself or think.

"I can't hear you. Can you call back with a better connection?" the girl asked. The call was ended.

Maddie was panicking. It was now or never.

What was wrong with the stupid phone? She had no clue and no time to figure it out. She took off running to Echo's house. It was her only shot.

As she ran across the park, she saw a couple leaning against a car. Chloe and Jake. *No, no, no. Not here. Not now. Not with dog pee all over me.* She diverted off the path, stepped in a hole, and went flying across the ground, scraping her face as she landed face down. She could feel blood dripping from her chin.

Maddie put her mind in automatic gear. Get up. Wipe the blood off. One foot in front of the other. She couldn't miss this chance. She made it to Echo's doorstep and managed to ring the bell. Blood was spewing from her chin into her hands. The world was spinning.

Mike answered the door. "Jesus Christ! Maddie, are you OK? Echo, come here now! Where's your brother? He'll know what to do."

"Don't ... please ... don't," Maddie murmured. "I just need to call my mom. I'll be fine. " Echo and her mother arrived at the doorway.

"What happened?" Echo cried.

"Can I use your phone? Please, Echo."

Echo handed Maddie her phone. Maddie dashed into the house, down the hall, and into the restroom.

JUST DO IT! NOW! You're going to make that call if it's the last thing you do.

She punched in the numbers, noticing she was

smearing blood all over Echo's phone.

"I need to page someone," she said into the phone, cupping her hand to muffle her voice. "Sure, what's the name?" the familiar female voice asked. "I think you called before."

Maddie ignored the blood puddling on the tile floor. "Ura DesGrace ... I need you to page Ura DesGrace."

"OK, just a second, please."

Maddie listened closely. "You're a disgrace," she heard over the loudspeaker.

Mission complete.

*

Elmo cleaned up Maddie's chin and placed a dressing on it. He didn't think she needed stitches, and Maddie reassured them all she was OK. She didn't need any more attention drawn to her tonight. She stuck to her story – a dog with gold hair had chased her, and she fell.

Lexie asked if she'd like to stay for dinner or if she wanted to be dropped off at home. Whatever was cooking here smelled so good. Maddie realized she was starving.

Echo's house was always the place to go for a good meal. Everyone sat at the oversized dining table, chatting and laughing while they filled their bowls. Maddie devoured the delicious food.

Why don't I have a family like this?

"What do you get when you cross a cell phone

with a skunk?" Mike began. Dad jokes – his favorite. He looked around the table. No one said a word. "Stinky service!" he called out, loudly laughing at his own joke.

"Why was the cell phone wearing glasses?" he continued.

Echo rolled her eyes. "Dad ..."

"Cuz ... he lost his contacts." Mike cracked up. No one else did. He regained his composure. "Seriously, I have a soft spot in my heart for phones and computers because my son is a tech wizard, and he's headed to MIT the first of the year to make us all proud ... why, he's already invented a phone system that ..."

"Dad ... nobody cares," Elmo cut him off. "Besides, I had to sign a disclosure, remember?"

I wonder if Plain Face Grace broke down and cried. I hope so. Knowing her, though, she's trying to protect her parents from feeling sorry for her ... what kind of person doesn't tell their mother, who's a doctor, that she probably has diabetes?

Dinner was over, so the girls went to Echo's room.

"Spill the tea, chica," Echo ordered once she got her bedroom door closed. Maddie threw herself across Echo's bed and recounted the evening.

"And the dog chased you?" Echo asked. Maddie sighed. "Well, kind of."

"That's bad, Mad ... I mean, really bad ..." Echo said.

Maddie laughed. "I know. But lucky I don't need stitches on my face. Then I'd look like a freak."

"No ... I mean, what you did to Grace. It's mean, bad ... savage ... in a bad way," Echo wasn't laughing. "When you think about it, Grace hasn't done anything to deserve you being so mean."

Maddie was furious. How dare Echo blatantly disrespect her? "Oh, yes, she did."

"What? What has she ever done to deserve all this?"

"I never told you this, but when Dad left, she and her parents used to have us over every Sunday ... we even went to church with them," Maddie spouted furiously. "Then Mom's drinking got out of control, and boom! That was the end of that. They kicked us out. Made us feel like freaks."

"But that was her parents' doing, not hers."

"She pitied me, Echo," Maddie continued. "But she's the pitiful one with her ugly face and stupid clothes. Plus, she has a crush on Jake ... remember?"

Maddie was exhausted, mentally and physically. She wanted to punch Echo in the face. She wanted her best friend to relish in the moment with her. She had pulled off the prank of a lifetime, and she wanted her victory celebration. Mostly though, she just wanted to go home. So, she told Echo she had to leave and snuck out the front door.

All the way home, the gold phone was lighting up and vibrating. She could see the yellow and red flashes going off inside her purse. She slipped inside and upstairs without Ashley coming out of her room. Thank God Mom wasn't home yet. Once she was safely inside with the door shut, she pulled the flashing phone out.

"You've gone too far," the message read.

She scoured the screen to see who the message was from, but there was no sender information. The phone went off again.

"You'll never get away with this," a new message read.

There were so many of these messages. Maddie stuck the phone under the stack of pillows on her bed. She gathered Shadow and sat on the bed to catch her breath and collect her thoughts.

What is going on with this phone? I think it's possessed. Who's texting me? Echo? Kaitlyn or Sophia? Elmo? Nancy? Grace? Maybe I'm just going crazy.

She couldn't help looking at the phone again.

"You will not get away with this."

"Why are you so mean?"

"Be sure your sins will find you out."

Maddie began to fear that whoever it was that was sending the messages was right.

EIGHTEEN

T he following morning, Maddie awoke to the phone flashing beside her. She texted back, "Leave me alone, loser!" but the text auto-corrected itself. It read: "Please leave me alone, XXX."

What is wrong with this stupid phone? It changes texts, and the phone beeps things out. It's like it's censored ... it is *censored!*

More messages were coming in: "You just wouldn't quit."

Sophia? She was beginning to get a little too outspoken. Maybe she was the culprit. Echo – after her little guilt trip last night? Are they all doing it together, teaming up on me?

The bedroom door burst open.

"Mad, you've got to see this." Ashley grabbed Maddie's arm and quickly ran downstairs to the living room, pointing at the local news on the television.

"We take you now to Sheriff Ben Kirby in Pine Cove," the news reporter said.

Ben Kirby was standing in front of the police

station downtown. "This is a town commonly thought of as a perfect small town with model citizens, a small community that, until now, has gone years without seeing one person in the jailhouse. But those days are over ... hear me out. A fourteen-year-old girl, Grace Harwood, has gone missing and foul play is heavily suspected. Trust me, there's a new sheriff in town, and he – I – am on this like a fly on honey. Anyone who knows of Grace's whereabouts or has any information about her is urged to contact authorities. Help us bring Grace home."

The reporter interrupted, and the TV cameras showed The Birdhouse restaurant.

"This is the restaurant in the tiny town of Ophir where Grace Harwood was last seen last night at about 7.30 pm. She went there with her family to meet a boy, Hayden Hanson, age sixteen, whom she had met online. Mr. Harwood said that when the boy didn't show up, his daughter excused herself to go to the restroom and never returned. The family believes the setup was linked to bullying incidents at her school. It is not known if foul play is involved in the disappearance or if Grace became so distraught that she ran off."

Mr. Harwood appeared on the television, looking noticeably upset. "Grace is a good girl. We thought she just went to the restroom to collect herself. She left her phone on the table, so we never suspected anything until ... she never returned. We drove around and looked everywhere. Please, if you know where Grace is, her mother, brother, and I beg you, let us know. We need our Gracie back."

The reporter began showing more clips of Grace, including her and Jackson singing together by the campfire. Maddie couldn't take another minute of it. The baby was crying. It was so loud! The room was spinning around in circles. She felt as if she would suffocate.

"Maddie, what happened to your face?" Ash asked. She was bouncing Liam on her hip.

Oh yeah, the dressing.

"Long story. Dog. Fell over," Maddie muttered.

"What's going on? What did you do? I'm your sister ... I'm all you have. Talk to me!"

Maddie couldn't think. She couldn't feel. It was Christmas Eve, and Grace was missing. She was never meant to go missing.

There was a knock on the door. Ashley went to answer it while Maddie flew up the stairs. She ran to her room and threw the phone into the closet, where it continued to flash and buzz. "Maddie, Ben needs to talk to you," Ashley yelled up the stairs.

She threw on some clothes. Her heart was pumping hard as she walked back down.

You can do this. Stay composed. Stay innocent. You can do this.

The sheriff was standing at the end of the stairway. "Maddison, good morning ... well, not really, but for formalities."

"Uh ... good morning."

Stay calm.

"Maddie, I am going to need to take you down to the station," Sheriff Kirby said. "Your mother will be meeting us there. I will need you to bring your tablet."

"Oh ... OK," Maddie replied. She returned with her tablet and was ushered into the back door of the police car.

The drive was just two blocks, but it felt like an eternity.

I never meant for it to go this far. Grace is sick, and no one even knows ... except Hayden. I mean, me.

Down at the station, Elodie was waiting. The sheriff led them to a small stale-smelling room and plastered a sign on the door: Interview in Progress – DO NOT DISTURB. Then he shut the door.

"The tablet," he said in Texas monotone, holding out his big, rough hand. Maddie passed it to him.

Thank God I deleted all the evidence. Guess I'm not so dumb after all.

"Well, Maddie," Ben began. "I guess you know by now that Grace Harwood is missing." Maddie looked up, sad-eyed. "I heard that on the news."

"I'm sure you have guessed by now that you are one of our prime suspects," the sheriff continued. "Truth be told, you're our *only* suspect. I'm going to send your tablet to our computer tech so he can investigate it."

The sheriff picked up his desk phone and dialed a number. "Katie, please come and get this tablet and get Elmo on the phone. Tell him I need him to come down to the station immediately."

Maddie's eyes widened. *Elmo? Her very own almost-brother. Would he betray her? Of course, he would.*

The secretary called back right away. Ben answered. "Oh ... well, that's right where he needs to be ... looking for her. Thank you for making the call."

Maddie sat stiffly in the straight wooden chair. The sheriff was perched directly across the table from her in his padded leather office chair. Her mom was in the corner.

"I have spoken with the Harwood family this morning," Sheriff Kirby told Maddie. "It seems Grace was strung along by a series of messages from a boy in California ... or a persona of a boy in California ... created for malicious purposes. You need to tell us everything you know." Maddie thought about what the sheriff was saying. If she did confess, she was in big trouble. If she didn't, she would be in even bigger trouble if she was caught. But, as long as there was a thread of hope she could slide by unscathed, she was going to risk it. She thought of at least telling him about Grace's health condition. But he would want to know how she knew. Then, she would have to tell him she was Hayden. It wasn't even so much about saving herself at this point. She was becoming more and more convinced by a gut feeling that she was the only one who could save Grace.

She was worried sick about Grace, and she would try and figure that out later, but going to jail would only complicate things even more. Besides, it terrified her just to think of being locked up.

"I don't know any ... anything about anything," Maddie lied. She caught herself wiggling around in her chair and forced herself to stop so she wouldn't give herself away. "I see how it's going to be," Sheriff Kirby said with disgust. "You'd better hope they find her alive, Maddison. Otherwise, you very well may be charged with ... murder."

Maddie gasped. She had seen plenty of crime television shows. They always asked for an attorney. But, unfortunately, the only attorney around Pine Cove that she knew of was Grace's father.

I'm screwed!

"Where were you the night of the twenty-third ... last night?" Ben asked.

"I was at Echo's house having dinner with her and her family. You can ask them."

Ben got on the phone again. "Katie, call the Blaze family residence. We need to check Echo's phone as well."

Maddie's stomach dropped. She needed to get onto Echo somehow – would she be smart enough to wipe her phone call log? The Birdhouse number would be in there. But she had no way of contacting her. Could she even trust Echo anymore, anyway?

Things were getting way too deep.

"I don't have enough evidence to hold you *yet*, Maddison," the sheriff said. "But ... I will.

Trust me; I will. Elodie, you are free to take her home. Maddison, we'll be meeting again." Maddie nodded. She couldn't say a word. Even if she could, she didn't want to. She just wanted to fade away ... far, far away.

*

At home, Elodie made a drink and sent Maddie to her room. Maddie immediately checked the gold phone, which was still going nuts.

It was Christmas Eve. She thought of children around the world waiting for Santa. She thought of Baby Liam. But mostly, Maddie thought of Grace. What if she'd been kidnapped or something? What if it was nothing to do with Maddie at all? But what if it was? It was freezing outside. If she had gone into the woods, there were bears. What about her diabetes? What would happen if she fainted? She fell into a fitful sleep, waking to messages all night.

"You should never have done it," one read.

"She just wanted to be your friend."

"You have time to make amends."

"Act now before it's too late. Tell the truth."

Just hang on, Grace. I will find you if it's the last thing I do ... and it just might be.

NINETEEN

If Grace is dead, I killed her.

With every passing moment, it was becoming more apparent that Grace probably *was* dead. If she were, there would be no question as to who had killed her. Maddie had. She knew it. Her friends knew it. And now her family, Grace's parents, and the sheriff knew it too.

Maddie couldn't shake the reality as she sat on her bed. Clutching her long slender legs, she nervously rocked back and forth.

If she is dead, my life will be over! She thought, not even aware of the irony.

Grace Harwood was missing. No teenager would run away and not take their phone.

Something terrible has happened. If only Maddie hadn't pushed Grace over the edge. How had it all gotten so far out of control?

What have I done?

It was Christmas Day, and she still wasn't found. Grace's photo was plastered all over the TV station report. Maddie watched with a feeling of dread.

Grace would never do that to her parents and her little brother ... not on purpose.

Maddie started to get dressed in warm clothes. She had to get out there and start looking. Her sketchpad was in her underwear drawer, where she'd stashed it away from prying eyes. She flicked through the pages distractedly. It seemed like years since she'd had the time and peace of mind to sketch freely. All these fashion ensembles – cute but nonpractical for hiking in the mountains looking for a lost person. Was this seriously her life now? Her collage of the Scarlet Squad. Were they still her friends? Were they the ones texting her? Would they betray her if the cops talked to them? A sketch of the town – oh yeah, the Happy Place from Grace's poem.

The Happy Place. Grace's happy place! Maybe that's where she could have headed?

She had to let someone know. She didn't even care what trouble she was in anymore. She grabbed the gold phone and called the number for the police station. It was no good – as soon as she tried to speak, her voice was beeped out, and the phone just flashed red non-stop.

Useless! What use is a phone if I can't even use it for an emergency!

"Mom?" Maddie called out, rushing out of her room, "Ash?" She needed to borrow one of their phones. But no one was home. It was Christmas, and the house was empty. What was going on?

Ash's car was in the driveway, but Mom's was gone. Maddie had to get to the mountain ASAP. Find the search team. Tell them about the happy place. Ashley had given her a crash course in driving in case of emergencies with Mom ... but not in a standard. She knew nothing about shifting gears. *I can't kill myself in a car wreck looking for Grace.*

But Maddie *was* a good driver – of ATVs. All those days spent racing Echo and Elmo on the trails on the mountain. She took off and ran as hard as she could towards Echo's house.

She cut through town. Twinkle lights and baubles mocked her on Main Street, and Christmas trees flashed brightly through windows. Families should be waking up, opening presents, eating food ... Warm. Inside. Together.

Echo's house was deserted as well. They usually went to their grandparents' house in Grand Junction, three hours' drive away. But Maddie bet Elmo at least would be out searching the woods.

Maddie lifted a small amount of soil from the pot plant on the third step and grabbed the spare key. She quickly unlocked the door and went straight to the wooden key holder that hung in the hall. Each key was labeled. She silently thanked the Blazes for being so organized and neat. Does borrowing an ATV in an emergency count as theft? There was no time for second thoughts. She rushed through the kitchen to the garage. The ATVs were all lined up, side by side. She moved Echo's ATV onto the driveway, closed the garage door, and sped off down the street and across town towards Miramonte Lake. The roads were empty. She passed the Ice Hut and thought of Jake. *Was he out looking for Grace, too? If I went missing, would he even care? Would anyone?*

Maddie arrived at the lake. She knew there was a dirt road that led up the mountain. She had been there with Echo's family tons of times, but she never paid attention to how they got there. A truck came flying past. Maddie whipped the steering wheel to the right to avoid getting hit. A thick cloud of dust blinded her. When she looked up, she was headed right into the lake.

Swerve! Swerve!

She turned as hard as she could, narrowly escaping plunging into the freezing water. Her heart was racing. Her palms were sweating to the point she could barely hold onto the steering wheel.

You can do this. You have *to do this.*

She saw a familiar fork in the road. "If we ever get separated, this is where we meet," Mike always told them when they came out to ride.

A sign read: The "Crossroads".

Maddie had no idea which way to go. She had never been religious. But for some reason, talking with God was the only thing she could think to do.

OK, God. I'm sure you're mad at me right now, but

this is for Grace. I know she believes in You, so ... here goes. If You help me find her, I'll change everything about my life. I'll be nice to Grace and kind to other people too. I promise ... please, just help me find her.

In a split-second decision, she took the pathway to the right.

The trail was rough with huge dips. The ATV was bottoming out. It was barely chugging up the steep ridge.

Come on ... come on ... we can do this.

A memory flashed before her. It was Grace's birthday party, and she was there. The children were playing hide-and-go-seek. It was Grace's turn to hide. She was good at hiding – patient and quiet, unlike the others. All the kids were looking for her, but Maddie was the one who had found her.

Where were all the rescuers? Where was the search team? Maddie had assumed she'd find everyone straight away and just be able to tell them about the happy place and the cave. Then she glanced around at the thick trees. Although not the largest mountain in the area, at this moment, Black Bear Mountain seemed quite large. What had she been thinking? The search team could be anywhere. Grace could be anywhere. Maddie was on her own.

Her mind buzzed through the chat conversations she'd had with Grace. *Lock-in... summer camp... lake by the cabin.* Maybe all the searchers would be there – her family would know about the cabin and church camps. She'd been to a lake up here once, with Echo's family. They'd driven part-way up and walked the rest of the way because the terrain was too steep and rocky. Finally, they'd hiked to a little lake called 'Rainbow Trout' where they had a picnic. It was years ago, but she remembered how beautiful it was ... and far. Could she find it again?

There was a giant chunk out of the dirt road. Maddie swerved, but it was too late. The tire went right into the hole ... and stuck. She pushed on the gas pedal as hard as she could, but all the wheel did was spin. The ATV was stuck.

Maddie pulled her phone out of her purse. Did maps even work here? There were over a dozen messages, with more coming every few minutes.

"It didn't have to be this way."

"Why are you so mean?"

"Have you learned your lesson and see being kind is the only way forward?"

She ignored the messages. The phone had no service already – it couldn't locate her on the map. She knew she'd have to take off on foot, but she had to decide which way to go. Where was the cabin? Where was the lake? Where was Grace?

"You could have had it all ..." a new message read. It had a clickable icon of a heart next to it. Maddie touched the heart, and a video began to play.

It was her. She was a little girl crouched down by a tree at the park. She was crying. "What's wrong? Are you sad, Maddie?" young Grace asked. Maddie looked up into the little girl's big, brown, kind eyes. "Yes ... I am ... I am very sad. My daddy went away and is never coming back."

The little girl sat down beside her. "I'm so sorry. My name is Grace. I will be your friend. Together, we will be all right. Friends can't make bad things go away, but they can make things better."

The two girls walked over to the playground in the park. They began to swing.

What the hell? Who sent that? Am I going crazy? Did this really happen? I think I remember ... I think it did. It was the first time I ever met Grace. I didn't like the way she asked me about my feelings. It was easier to ignore them. But I think we ended up having a fun time.

When the video ended, Maddie realized she was using up precious cell phone battery time. She had to get moving, so she grabbed her coat and a bottle of water, then slid the gold phone into her purse and strapped it across her shoulders.

The track was so steep. Her legs felt weak. She caught her breathe and stumbled on. Why hadn't she eaten something this morning?

Is Grace even on the mountain? Is she even alive? Where is the search team?

She trudged up higher and higher, struggling to get her footing on the rocky surface. She began to cry. She hated crying. It was so weak.

Grace is probably dead, and it's all my fault.

Then she saw it in the distance - the lake and, right beside it, a cabin.

Maybe there is a God.

Maddie found the strength to put one foot in front of the other until she made it to the cabin. The sun was nearly setting. She opened the cabin door and fell inside. "Grace? Hello? Anyone?"

Inside it was dark and quiet, obviously empty. Where on earth were the searchers?

Maddie found an oil lantern and a book of matches next to it. Glorious light filled the cabin. The place was nice and clean. It was a one-room log cabin with bunk beds along the wall. There was a kitchen with a potbelly iron stove and a cupboard full of canned goods. She was so hungry. But the sun was going down. Surely Grace wouldn't survive another night if she was out there.

She pulled out the useless phone. She wanted to text Ashley to let her know she was OK and wouldn't be home. No point stressing them all out on Christmas Day. But she still had no service. So how were these texts coming? There was a new one:

"You could have had it all ... and you still can. It is all at your fingertips." There was another heart icon. Maddie automatically clicked on it.

The video resumed where the story had left off. Maddie, Grace, Echo, Sophia, Kaitlyn, and Arkadia were tweens. They were having a slumber party at Maddie's house. Maddie's mother came in, drunk.

"You girls have a good night," she told them and then walked out. Maddie rolled her eyes. Grace hugged her. "She'll come around one day, at least I hope she will. But you know what? All the tough times you've been through with your mom and dad have made you the strong and kind girl you are today. And I *like* that girl!" The others gathered around Maddie. "So do we!" they cried in unison. They had a group hug.

I am going insane. I have lost my ever-lovin mind. I'm hallucinating.

It was no time to get weak. She had to stay strong. She had a quick drink of water and headed back out into the dark and cold, lantern in hand. She took a moment to clear her mind, looking down at the twinkling lights of the town below.

Wait a minute ... the town below. Grace's poem. This was the spot. She was right. There was a rocky outcrop through the trees there – could the cave be in there somewhere?

"Grace? Are you out there?" Maddie yelled.

She ran through the trees, branches whipping her, the lantern throwing frightening shadows around her. *Do not think about bears.* She reached the section of rocks – a cliff face towering over her. She held the lantern up. There was a darker section – a gap. A narrow cave. She ran to the entrance and looked inside.

Maddie screamed. She could not believe what she was seeing. Grace's lifeless body was curled up inside the cave.

TWENTY

"Oh my god, Grace! Grace!" Maddie screamed. Falling to her knees, she began to sob. The tears wouldn't stop. "WAKE UP!" she begged. "I promise everything will be different." Maddie took her Grace's hand. It was cold. "I didn't mean it. I'm sorry. Please, Grace ... "

Grace didn't move. She shook gently, no change. *What have I done? If Grace is dead, I will kill myself. I cannot live with the guilt. Who have I become?*

Maddie started to rock back and forth, back and forth, sobbing harder and harder and gasping for breath. "Grace, I am sorry I was so mean to you. I don't hate you. I hate myself." She touched her once more, softly as though she was stroking baby Liam.

She felt Grace's hand. Her finger moved ... ever so slightly.

"Grace! Are you alive?" Maddie asked, panicked. "You are ... I think you are." Grace fluttered one eye open and then fell back unconscious.

"You're alive, Grace. Stay with me," Maddie

begged. "I am going to get you home ... just stay with me."

Maddie picked up Grace and carried her, step by step, back to the cabin. She laid her on the sofa and covered her with the wool blanket.

Her blood sugar is probably too low ... or too high. She could be dehydrated too. How do I know? What do I do?

She had to choose, so she ran into the kitchen and poured some water into a cup. Then she hurried into the living room and sat Grace up.

"Grace ... take a drink."

Grace's eyes rolled back in her head, but Maddie kept on until Grace managed a tiny sip. Then she took another. And after a while, she began to come to.

"You need to drink this so you don't pass out again."

A puzzled look fell over Grace's pale face. "You ... you were Hayden all along. I should have known no guy would like me like that. You are the one who paged the restaurant and called me Disgrace. You ..." Her voice was trailing as she slipped out of consciousness again. "I am so sorry, Grace," Maddie said, tears streaming down her face.

She was rousing a bit. "I know I am a nerd. I know my clothes aren't fashionable. I know I'm not cool. I am a disgrace."

"That's not true," Maddie said desperately. "You're so smart. Your family loves you so much.

You're a poet and the most amazing singer I've ever heard." Maddie paused. "I was jealous of you."

Maddie pulled out the phone and dialed Ash, then her Mom, then Echo. No service. No one to come and help them.

Another message came through. All it contained was a heart. Maddie clicked on the heart, and another video appeared.

The girls were older now. They were sitting around, talking about their club and the kids at school. "I noticed a new girl who looks like she could use a friend," Maddie said. "Should we invite her to be in the club?"

"Sure," the girls agreed. Grace smiled and added, "That's what it's all about ... kindness gone full-circle."

There was only 5% battery left on the phone.

A flash of lightning made Maddie jump. In an instant, it was pouring rain.

OK. Think. It's night. It's raining. It's cold. Grace is super weak. We've got no way of communicating with the outside world.

Maddie tucked the blanket tighter around Grace. She looked so fragile and sickly. Maddie wondered how she could ever be so mean to someone so weak. *It's like picking on Baby Liam.* Her heart wrenched at the thought of such a thing.

She opened a can of soup, heated it, and woke Grace up again, convincing her to drink it. "I'm going to get you back to your parents as soon as I can. But we can't go anywhere tonight. I'll build a fire, and we'll wait here until morning, and the rain is over."

Grace looked blankly at her. Maddie worried that she was still in a blood sugar daze but had no time to think about it. She put logs in the wood-burning stove and threw twigs on top like she had seen Echo's dad do when they went camping. Then she found a match and lit it up.

Whew! Thank heavens. Oh, and thank YOU, God. Please help me get Grace home safely. Her thoughts went back to the Crossroads and her deal with God. *Maybe ... just maybe He's real.* Grace was alive, and Maddie had to figure out how to keep her that way. The fire was warming up the room. The rain was deafening on the roof. Maddie heated up some soup for herself and wrapped a blanket around her shoulders. Her whole body ached and begged her for sleep, but she kept herself awake all night, sitting up by Grace's side, checking she was breathing and topping up the fire.

*

Maddie must have dozed off in the early hours of the morning and woke up with a start to an icy cold cabin. The fire had gone out. Grace was OK, breathing steadily, and color had returned to her face. The sun was rising, and the rain had stopped.

It was time to go home, but first, she knew they both needed some strength. Maddie boiled the tea kettle on the stove and fixed two bowls of packet oatmeal and two steaming mugs of hot cocoa. She woke Grace up, and they ate.

"What happened that night?" Maddie asked. "Sorry, you don't have to tell me if you don't want to. Were you trying to get up to the cabin?"

"It's alright. I don't mind," Grace replied. "At first, I always managed to deal with you and the Scarlet Squad not liking me - even kind of hating me. I knew you didn't know me, so you couldn't hate me. You just thought you did ... or wanted to ... or something. But as time went on and the bullying got worse, I couldn't see how to make it stop. "

"There was only one way out."

"Hayden was the first boy I've ever liked, like a boyfriend. I told him secrets. Well, I guess I told *you* the secrets."

Grace was quiet for a few minutes as if it was soaking in all over again. Maddie could see the pain on her face and felt guilty.

"When the announcement was made and I realized the joke was on me, I began to figure out that there was no Hayden after all. I didn't want my parents to see me upset, mostly my mom. She has a hard enough job being a doctor without feeling sorry for me. Besides, I just wanted to die. I couldn't take any more of the hateful comments and snide remarks. So, I left the restaurant, grabbed a lantern from the path by the restaurant door and ran to the only place

I could go to think. Should I kill myself? If I was going to, I wanted it to be at my happy place. But I never made it that far."

"Oh, Grace. I'm so sorry. You were so brave to come up here in the dark. Can you walk?" Maddie asked. She was thinking of her hike the day before. Was Grace up to it? The restaurant and Ophir were on the other side of the mountain and much closer to the cabin than Pine Cove, and Grace had only just made it. How would she get Grace down the mountain?

Grace tried to stand, but her legs gave way. "That's OK, don't worry," Maddie said.

Think, think.

She scouted around the outside of the cabin, looking for anything that might help. There was a wheelbarrow. One of the wooden wheels had a chunk out of it, so it bumped with every movement.

"OK, Grace, this may hurt, but we have to get you in here," Maddie said. She pulled the wheelbarrow as close as she could and spread the wool blanket out inside. "Come on." Maddie used her strength to sit Grace up. Then, she pulled her up, and she practically fell into the barrow.

"Ouch!" Grace cried when her head hit the side.

"You're OK," Maddie coached. She hated to hurt Grace even more, but there was no other way. Maddie put her coat on and tossed her purse over her shoulder. She grabbed an extra blanket from one of the bunk beds and tucked it in over Grace. "Hold tight."

"Ready?" Grace nodded. "Yes."

It seemed so surreal. Maddie was pushing Grace Harwood in a dilapidated wheelbarrow down Black Bear Mountain.

I'm going to wake up soon and be late for school. Surely this is not really happening.

Every bump made Grace wince. Although she never complained, Maddie knew it hurt. "Hang in there. You're doing well." She struggled to push the old wheelbarrow across the rough rocks, but she didn't want Grace to know. She was sure Grace didn't want to be a burden, so she pretended it was easier than it was.

"Why, Maddie?" She heard Grace speak up after what felt like hours. "Why were you so mean to me? We used to be friends when we were little, and then you suddenly hated me."

Maddie stopped pushing for a minute. It sounded so dumb, even in her head. "Because I ... well, because I wanted to be in the popular group ... to hang out with Chloe and them. I knew they wouldn't have anything to do with me if I was playing with you, so..."

"Yeah ... I never wanted to hang out with them," Grace admitted. "They never seemed like good friends to have. You were ... when we were little. I was never sure what I did to make you hate me. I liked being friends with you."

"I liked being friends with you too, Grace. Your family was really nice to us after my dad left. I remember going to church with you and going to your house for Sunday dinner. Then I guess your parents got tired of my mom." Maddie hoped she wasn't saying too much, but it seemed a good time to air the laundry.

Grace shook her head. "Oh no, Maddie. That's not what happened. My parents wanted to keep helping your mom. But she took offense at something. She said she wanted no part of us or our church and didn't want her girls around us. I remember crying when I heard her say that. I loved you coming over and going to church with me."

Maddie was silent. The hill was sloping downwards. It was hard to hold the weight of the wheelbarrow from pulling her down. They crunched over the wet rocks and muddy track.

Suddenly, there was a rustling in the bushes. Maddie caught a shadow out of the side of her eye. She froze and took another look. It was a large black bear. Frantically, she tried to recall the lessons at school about what to do in the event of a bear encounter. Living near Black Bear Mountain, from kindergarten through high school, bear safety was taught. But ... she was blank. The bear was creeping down from the bushes towards them. It looked curious and probably hungry too. He was enormous.

"Grace, stay still."

She remembered Elmo telling her that if you weren't big and bad enough to tangle with a bear, leave him alone. "You either freeze and let him walk away, or you'll have to confront him. It's fight or flight," he had said.

But this bear wasn't going away. She had to be bigger and badder than he was.

She glanced around for a rock or a stick, but there weren't any good ones nearby. She looked at her purse. The phone was blinking.

Maybe ....

She pulled it out and flashed the light in the bear's face. It did nothing – he kept coming closer. "You can kill me, but don't you dare touch Grace," Maddie screamed. She took a couple of quick steps towards the bear, channeling her mom as she wound back her arm and threw the gold phone as hard as she could straight at it. The phone hit the bear square on the snout. "She's done nothing wrong. Leave her alone!" Maddie continued, charging another few steps forward.

The bear turned and ran away.

At last, the stupid phone was good for something!

Maddie was shaking like a leaf. She'd never felt so much adrenaline.

I've got to get us out of here.

She grabbed the wheelbarrow handles and took off, too fast, down the muddy slope. She pulled back, but the weight was too much – they were sliding, she was tripping, and then they were both tumbling on the rocks… everything went black.

TWENTY-ONE

Oh, God. Everything feels broken.

Maddie opened her eyes. Her face was in the mud. Her hands, knees, head: everything felt battered and grazed.

Grace was sprawled beside her, shivering. The wheelbarrow had smashed.

"C'mon, girl ... we can do this," Maddie said. She didn't know if she was talking to herself or Grace. She stood up, mustered all the strength she had, and hauled Grace to her feet. With her arm around Grace's waist, she half supported her, half hoisted her through the mud and tumbled rocks. *The ATV must be close now. We'll find help soon.*

Grace didn't say a word for a few long minutes until she finally managed to speak. "You don't hate me anymore, do you?" she asked.

"I never hated you," Maddie answered. "I just thought I did. I think I hated myself."

There it was! The ATV stuck in the pothole. Was it seriously only yesterday she'd left it here?

Maddie sat Grace down and walked over to the ATV. She started the engine and began to rock the bike, throwing it in first gear as she did. This had to work – there was no other option. She throttled the gas full force, and the ATV popped out of the hole.

Finally, something was going right.

Maddie helped Grace onto the back of the quad bike. She hoped Grace could hold on tight enough as they started the long journey down the incline. Maddie skilfully maneuvered the ATV across the rocky and muddy terrain. Since yesterday, the track had changed – there must have been some flash flooding with the storm last night. The rain dug out whole sections, and the trail was littered with debris and sliding rocks. Down below, she could see the Crossroads. There were people and vehicles. The searchers!

When she got closer, Maddie could see the issue. The damage to the track was severe – there was a sharp drop-off at the Crossroads. They couldn't get their trucks up it, and Maddie wouldn't be able to get the ATV down it. The searchers had seen her coming and were gathering on their low section of track. Elmo was there.

Maddie drove to the edge. "Elmo! I've got Grace! She needs help!"

Elmo strode through the mud towards them with Grace's parents and Jackson close behind him. Maddie helped Grace off the back of the ATV and lowered her as gently as she could down the steep slope into the waiting arms. Grace was ushered away towards a medical team waiting in a truck.

Relief flooded through Maddie, and her knees gave out. She sat down heavily at the top of the slope, looking at the drop of a few feet as if it was Mt Everest. There was simply no way she could get down there by herself. She guessed she'd have to stay here forever.

"Mad!" someone called out. A small group of people bundled up against the cold were coming towards her. Was that Mom? Ash? Nancy?

"Thank God you're OK. We were so scared. We've been looking for you." Maddie felt hands reaching for her and supporting her, lifting her down.

"I found your sketch," Ash was talking. "We guessed you'd gone up the mountain. They sent a drone over last night and saw the ATV and the smoke from the cabin. But no one could get there with the flash flooding. Are you OK?"

"Yeah," Maddie said quietly. She had no energy to talk.

"Where'd you find her? We'd searched the cabin already," Nancy was saying. "In a cave ... long story ... near the cabin."

"How on earth did you get her down?" Her mom was squeezing Maddie too tight. She could barely breathe.

Maddie just shook her head. There was something else she wanted to say. "I took one of your gold phones," she muttered to Nancy.

Nancy put her arm around Maddie compassionately. "We'll get to all that later. Right now, I'm just glad you're both OK."

A police car pulled up, lights flashing. Sheriff Kirby stepped out.

This is where I go to jail. Isn't it?

TWENTY-TWO

It was the best day of Maddie's life.

It was the worst day too.

Maddie sat, shivering with fear, in the stiff wooden chair in the interrogation room. She had been there before, but she hadn't found it nearly as serious then as she did now. Not even an hour earlier, she had successfully delivered Grace back to her family. Now, she was sitting in a tiny room in a whole lot of trouble. The medical team had checked her out at the Crossroads, and remarkably, she wasn't too busted up. A few scrapes and bruises. Nothing to send her to hospital. She had a clean blanket around her shoulders, but despite her mom and sister's best efforts, she hadn't been allowed to go home to shower or clean up.

"I need to inform you of your rights, Maddison," Sheriff Kirby began. "You have the right to remain silent. Anything you say can and will be used against you in a court of law. Do you understand?"

"Yes, sir," Maddie replied in a quivering voice.

"Do you wish to speak to me about the matter at hand with Grace Harwood?"

Maddie thought about it. She had watched crime shows before. She knew she didn't have to talk. But it had all gone too far. She looked up. "Yes. I want to talk to you about Grace."

"The last we spoke, I had concerns about your tablet, if you recall," the sheriff drawled. Maddie nodded.

"You underestimated our technical abilities ... or that of Elmo if you will," he continued. "Elmo found an overwhelming amount of evidence on that tablet ... on the hard drive, that is. Messages to Grace under assumed names, which, by the way, is illegal in and of itself."

Maddie's blood was draining to her feet. It was growing hard to breathe.

"You had many warnings and opportunities to stop, but you were determined to bully that poor little girl. You know, and I know, she never did anything to you. Did she?"

Maddie opened her mouth, but no words came. She shook her head. He was right.

"Oh, and it doesn't end there," he went on. "I have a note you wrote to Grace in math class as physical evidence of bullying. Mrs. Motts has given it over to me. Mr. Freeman also had a world of information to share about your behavior. But we'll save all that for court. Now ... are you proud of yourself? Are you happy you have shamed your family? And that now you'll drag Grace and her family through the mire to relive this unspeakable crime and the cruel events leading up to it as you stand trial?"

Maddie managed a meek, "No, sir."

"Of course, you aren't ... but it's too late, little lady. It's too late. I need to inform you what you're being charged with."

Maddie looked up, afraid to ask.

Sheriff Kirby pulled out a stack of papers. "Theft of property, seven-fifty to two-thousand ... dollars, that is. They don't give cell phones away - in case you didn't know. They cost a pretty penny," he began. "Oh, and that's a Class 1 misdemeanor in Colorado ... six to eighteen months in jail and − or − five hundred to five thousand dollars in fines. So, what in the Sam Hill were you thinking, Miss Hunter?"

He drew a breath, shook his head furiously, and smiled as if he was enjoying being the bearer of bad news. Then he fumbled through the stack and pulled out the next page. "As I said before, cyberbullying is a crime in the state of Colorado and will not be tolerated in *my* town. Let's not forget harassment, which is bullying in person. And criminal mischief: the Harwoods' house and car ... criminal trespassing ... then, how many cars did you scratch, or tires did you slash? That's the destruction of property. We've plenty of witnesses. The judge will set a bond ... or maybe he'll deem you too dangerous even to have one.

You're in more trouble than you can shake a stick at."

With that, he slapped handcuffs on Maddie and led her down the cold, grey corridor of the police station to a small cell with peeling pink marshmallow-colored paint. *Pink!* She felt like it had been painted pink just to make her hurt a little more. He unlocked the door with his jingling keys, swung the door open, and ushered Maddie in.

The minute she stepped inside, he slammed the door shut. It echoed in her ears.

"Don't do the crime if you can't do the time," the sheriff grumbled as he disappeared down the hall.

Maddie looked around the six-by-six cell. She had never felt so alone. The room reeked of sadness and despair. There was a cement block with a makeshift flat plastic mat on it with a crumpled brown sheet on top. Was that meant to be a bed? A steel toilet and a rusted sink were built into the wall. The light was dim and flickering, as was Maddie's head.

*

The following day, Katie, the lady from the front desk, appeared at the gated door. She looked to be in her early thirties and wore her black hair in a bun atop her head. She never made eye contact as she handed a tiny box of cereal through a slit in the bars to Maddie, followed by a small carton of milk and a plastic spoon.

She acts like I have cooties. I guess, in a way, I do.

"Thank you," Maddie said, painfully aware of how disgusting she must look in her ripped plaid shirt and muddy jeans she'd been wearing for too many days to count. She was sure she didn't smell very good, either.

Maddie was nauseated but starving at the same time. As soon as she managed to get the bland bran cereal down, Katie returned. "Spoon?" she asked, holding out her hand. Maddie gave her the spoon. "Contraband," she warned, tossing it in a trash can that sat down the hall in the corridor. She returned a moment later. "You have a visitor."

She unlocked the gate then motioned for Maddie to come out. Maddie felt so disgusting. She became increasingly aware of how long it had been since she had a shower. She pushed it all to the back of her mind and followed Katie down the long hall to a small booth with a steel stool securely screwed into the cement floor. There was another stool just like it on the other side of the glass. She waited, expecting to see her mother, or maybe Ashley, at any moment. To her surprise, it was Nancy who had come to visit. Nancy smiled. "Oh, Maddie, I'm so sorry," she took a seat on the cold, hard stool. "I know it's tough in there. Trust me, I know."

Maddie wanted to burst out crying.

"It's OK to be ... well, to be not OK. It's all right to be scared. It's normal, in fact. It will all work out, but I can't say how or when. But it *will* work out, and I'll do all I can to help."

Maddie nodded. "Thank you ... but ... why?"

"Because I was where you are, Maddie," Nancy began. "I know I've told you that before, but I don't think you ever believed me. I was a mess. I was in a lot of trouble. Finally, it hit home, and I realized that all my anger was getting me nowhere. It was only hurting me. I had to work through my issues, not around them. I had to face it all head-on. It wasn't easy. But I did it. And now, my life is centered around helping others ... like you."

Maddie couldn't think of one thing to say. She was touched and embarrassed. But she was suspicious too. Maybe somebody sent Nancy to get more information for Ben Kirby.

She looked around awkwardly, her eyes landing on Nancy's wrist. "Nice tat," she said.

Nancy smiled at her butterfly tattoo. "Yeah, it really is. It's a reminder to enjoy life and to embrace kindness. You see what's under it?"

Maddie peered through the dirty glass, trying to see what Nancy was talking about. She could see a very faint scar.

"It's where I cut myself ... on purpose, Mad. I wanted to end it all that day and many other days too. When I finally found what I had been searching for, I decided to have a butterfly tattooed over the scar to remind me that there is life after despair. Don't ever forget that."

Nancy continued. "I do know that your life has been ... well, it hasn't been easy. Your dad left when you were just a little girl. Every little girl, and even big girls, needs a dad. I know your mother's an alcoholic. You needed her to be emotionally there for you. You've always needed that, and she has never been. And I also know your sister is the closest thing you have to a mother. I respect her for that. But she's a teen mom, a single teen mom herself. So, your life has not been easy.

"You feel abandoned. It's still up to you what you make of it, though, because you're the one behind bars when it all comes down to it. You're the one who will suffer the consequences of bad behavior or enjoy the consequences of good behavior. There are good consequences, just like there are bad ones. That is why I'm here. I'm here to help and share what I have learned." Maddie didn't know what to say. "Thank you," was all she could manage. "Thank you for coming."

"No problem," Nancy told her. "Let me just tell you what will happen. You'll have a detention hearing in the next few days. There's no doubt the decision will be to charge you because there are so many charges, some serious. Then you'll have a bond. Unfortunately, it will be high, so the chances are that you'll have to stay in jail until your trial. Since Pine Cove is such a small town and isn't properly equipped with a juvenile detention center, they must rush your court date. Normally for a juvenile, it's three months."

Maddie gasped.

"But as I said, I think your court date will be expedited."

"What will happen then?" Maddie asked. She didn't want to know, but she needed to prepare herself.

"That will be up to the judge and the jury unless you forfeit your right to a jury and just let the judge decide," Nancy said. "You'll be appointed an attorney because I know your mother can't afford one."

Maddie couldn't digest anymore, and Nancy knew it. "I wish there were more I could do," Nancy said. "I've bought some clothes here for you. They are just checking them over and will bring them to you shortly."

"Thank you." Maddie looked up and smiled. "I have a question before you go." She was nervous to ask, but she had to. "What was the deal with that phone? It was like all crazy ... beeping out things like a censor, sending messages that I have no idea who they're from, and playing videos like of Grace and me as kids and stuff."

Nancy stared. "Sorry. But I'm not sure I know what you're talking about."

"You know ... the messages about being kind and the videos of how things could have been ..." Maddie said. "But it wouldn't let me call anyone or use maps, even in an emergency."

Nancy shook her head. "What I mostly understand about how the phone works is that I don't understand.

Elmo and the other techies who invented it are genius-level communication and human behavioral scientists. I simply placed my order for a kindness phone because life is nothing without kindness. I think you are figuring that out. The phone is built on neuroscience. It reacts to brain waves and the stored energy of memories and possibilities. It can project new plans and override old ones. Elmo calls it a Cognitive Augmentation Influencer. I just know ... it can do miracles. In short ... it helps you make better choices by blocking bad behavior and promoting kindness instead. But, to answer your question ... no one was behind the text messages and videos except for you ... the reinvented version of you. Fortunately, you don't have to understand how it works for it to work. But it sounds like there are some issues. It's brand-new software. I'll tell Elmo what you said."

Maddie was trying to absorb what Nancy had said when Katie appeared. "Time's up," she said. Nancy gave Maddie a last smile and nod.

As Katie walked Maddie down the long hall to her cell, she could hear hollering down a side hall.

"Men. Keep walking," Katie instructed. Maddie obeyed Katie's order.

"Fresh meat!" she heard a man yell. "Fresh ... Maddie?"

Without thinking, Maddie looked down the side hall. She could see Samuel's head sticking out between the cell bars.

"Maddie, who'd ya kill?" he yelled.

"Quiet, or you'll go to solitary," Katie commanded, whisking Maddie down the main hall and around the corner to what Maddie now realized was the women's side. She wanted to throw up.

She hated Samuel for what he had done to her sister, and now she was no better because of what she had done to Grace.

Can it get any worse?

Maddie quickly learned that it could.

As Katie brought her to her cell, Maddie noticed someone was in the cell across from hers. It was a woman all curled up on a mat on the floor. She smelled like a bottle of vodka.

Oh ... no! No, no ... no.

The woman slurred something to Katie.

"Welcome home away from home," Katie said as she walked away.

Maddie was hoping she was wrong and that the drunk just looked and sounded like her mother. But no. It was her mother.

Elodie had just realized who was in the cell across the hall. "Maddison! You bad, bad girl."

Maddie wanted to block it all out. She wanted to hide, but there wasn't even a blanket to hide under. All she could do was sit there and listen to her mother rant.

"That no-good rat, Texas wannabe cowboy ... he got you and then went after me ... you have always found a way to mess up anything I ever had with any man ... even your dad. He didn't want kids, you know ... then he had one ... and then he had two ... and you were the straw that broke the camel's back, thank you very much. But then again, a *real* man would have stepped up to the plate and made the best of it. Not your father. He just left because that was the easy thing to do. I tried, Mad. I did try. But there is only so much pain and humiliation a woman can take. More than anything, I was determined to protect you girls."

With that, Elodie passed out again. Maddie replayed her mother's words in her head. She wanted to protect us. From what? Something wasn't making sense.

Katie was walking down the hall, but Maddie called her back. "Is there any way I can shower?"

Katie frowned. "I guess. You do need a shower." She let Maddie out and took her down the hall to a shower. No doors. It was an open shower. Anyone could see her. Maddie was quickly learning; there was no privacy in jail.

The water was only lukewarm, but it felt like heaven. Katie handed her a bar of pink soap. Was there no escape from that hated color?

Maddie didn't really care what color the soap was.

"Enough," Katie told her. She had never gone even two days without a shower. She was beginning to feel almost human.

Maddie turned the shower off, dried off, and put her new sweatpants and top on.

The two went back down the hall. Maddie was as quiet as she could be, hoping not to wake her mother up. But Elodie was gone.

"Where'd she go?" Maddie asked, pointing to the empty cell.

"The drunk? Probably slept her way out," Katie answered curtly. "Wouldn't be the first time." Maddie wondered if what Katie said was true.

She had to be indifferent. Nancy was right. Her life did suck. She deserved to have a real family like her friends, and even her enemies had. Then again, she deserved to have no family at all.

Back in her cell, Maddie's thoughts were racing.

How had she gotten to this point?

Maybe Nancy was right. Perhaps she was all screwed up because of her dad and her mom. But, on the other hand, she was undoubtedly correct that it didn't matter now. Even her mother was gone ... once again.

"Miss Hunter has an attorney here to see her," a male voice called.

Katie unlocked the door and motioned Maddie out. The two walked down the hall to a tiny room with two chairs. Katie waited until Maddie took a seat and then left the room. A young man with blue eyes, messy blond hair, and a funny-looking suit sat down beside her. "Maddie, I'm Peter Brown, Attorney at

Law," he said, sticking out his hand to shake hers. "I'm your court-appointed attorney."

Maddie didn't feel like talking. What could she say anyway?

"There was a detention hearing today, and you are being detained," he informed. "You have a cash bond of fifty thousand dollars."

The bond made no difference to Maddie. She knew she wasn't getting out anyway. "OK," she said.

"You do know what you're being charged with, don't you?" he asked, appearing as nervous as Maddie was.

"Yes, the sheriff told me." She said quietly.

"Well, the good news is that they dropped the trespassing and the criminal mischief. The bad news is that harassment, theft, and cyberbullying are serious charges. You may be looking at serving time in juvenile detention. I will do my best to represent you efficiently and get you off as light as possible. There is no guarantee, though. You may walk ... but you very well may not. I suggest you waive your rights to a jury trial. They'll fry you. You've turned this town upside down. Best to try to pull on the judge's heartstrings. Good luck with that."

"OK... this is my first time with all of this," Maddie told her lawyer. Mr. Brown laughed. "Yeah, mine too."

As he was leaving, he turned back around and wiped the sweat off his forehead. "Oh, and yes ... I almost forgot. Your court date is the day after tomorrow."

Maddie was taken back to her cell. She began to clean everything she could with her dirty laundry. Nothing looked different. Everything still stunk too. But it made her feel better in a weird sort of way.

That night, Maddie dreamed she was falling through a dark tunnel, spiraling out of control. She wanted to wake up so she could realize it had all been a bad dream and that everything was all right. But it wasn't. And maybe it would never be again.

TWENTY-THREE

Everything was a blur as Maddie was ushered in through a side door into the courtroom. Nothing seemed real. She was trembling so fiercely she could hardly walk as Mr. Brown led the way.

"Don't be nervous," he told her. "The worst that can happen is ... well, never mind that. Prepare for the worst and hope for the best."

Maddie was not comforted by her attorney's word or his lack of experience. She felt so small and vulnerable, looking out over the sea of people. She hadn't expected a crowd. It was supposed to be a trial before the judge. Maddie was grateful Nancy had brought up a black skirt, white blouse, and plain black shoes for her to wear. It was the kind of churchy outfit she had made fun of Grace for wearing in the past, but it was perfect for her day in court.

Everyone stood for the Honorable Judge, William Wilson, as he made his entrance.

Mr. Brown ushered Maddie before him. Maddie

tried not to think about how, as little girls, she and Ashley destroyed his treehouse.

Judge Wilson cleared his throat. "Maddison Hunter, do you understand you are being charged with Harassment, Cyberbullying, and Misdemeanor Theft Class 3?"

"Yes, sir."

"And do you understand that the state could also enhance your cyberbullying charges to cyberstalking and harassment through an electronic device?"

Maddie's head began to spin. "Yes, your Honor."

"And you have waived a jury trial of your peers?"

"Yes, sir."

"As you may have been informed, your case has made headlines in Pine Cove," the judge explained. "Many of the citizens have requested to observe and even make statements in the proceedings. I, of course, have obliged them."

Maddie struggled to breathe as Mr. Brown led her in front of the crowd to two chairs and a table where they took their places. Mr. Brown pulled out his battered briefcase and fumbled through the papers.

"I'd like to call the prosecution."

The District Attorney, Mack Shay, walked up to the podium. Maddie recognized the man. He was one of her mother's long string of boyfriends.

This can't be good.

She never realized he was an attorney, let alone the DA. He was confident and assertive as he thanked the judge and introduced the case.

"Ladies and gentlemen of the proud town of Pine Cove. I stand before you today to present the evidence and hear the testimonies that will prove to you, without a shadow of a doubt, that fourteen-year-old Maddison Hunter has committed heinous crimes against our community and the law-abiding citizens therein."

Judge Wilson took a drink of water. "Miss Hunter and Counselor Brown have opted to forego a jury of her peers. Instead, they have chosen to rely on my verdict to determine Miss Hunter's innocence or guilt and implement punishment if she is found guilty. We have stretched the court's scheduling to accommodate a speedy trial for this juvenile defendant. I hope that we work together to resolve this issue before the new year. I would like to call Echo Blaze to the witness stand now. Miss Blaze ..."

Maddie was shocked. She was way too nervous to look at who was in the courtroom. She never thought her friends would be there. She tried not to think of all the ways she had belittled Echo over the years. She hoped Echo's loyalty would prevail, but another look at the DA who was about to question her gave her little promise.

Echo took the oath and sat on the witness stand. She looked over at Maddie as if to tell her she was sorry for what she was about to say.

"How long have you known Maddison Hunter,

Miss Blaze?" the DA asked. Echo counted on her fingers. "Ten years, at least."

"Would you say you know her very well?"

"Yes."

"Did the defendant, you, Kaitlyn Randle, and Sophia Bradley have a club that you formed in the third grade?"

"Yes."

"And what was the name of the gang ... excuse me, group?"

"The ... Scarlet Squad."

"And who was the leader of ... the Scarlet Squad?" Echo didn't answer.

"Well, do you see her in the courtroom?"

"Yes, sir, I do."

"Will you point her out?"

Echo reluctantly pointed to Maddie.

"What did Grace Harwood ever do to Maddie to deserve the harsh bullying and cyberbullying Miss Hunter was implementing? What did she tell you the reason was?"

Echo was silent.

"Miss Blaze, may I remind you that you are under oath. You told authorities the reason Miss Hunter gave you, and now, under oath, you are being asked to repeat what Miss Hunter told you."

Echo began to cry. "She was born." Maddie shrunk down.

"Objection!" Mr. Brown roared, standing to his

feet with a vengeance.

The judge took his bifocals off and wiped his brow with a handkerchief. "To what?" Mr. Brown sat back down. "Never mind."

Echo was dismissed. As she walked to her seat in the crowded courtroom, she mouthed to Maddie, "I'm sorry."

Next, the DA called Jake Taylor to the stand.

Maddie wanted to crawl under her chair.

"Mr. Taylor, did you and the defendant, Miss Hunter, have a relationship at the beginning of the school year?"

"Yes, sir, we did have a *brief* relationship," Jake admitted.

The rose, the party, the dancing, the wonderful way he made her feel special. She missed his voice, his touch, and everything else about him. And she hated him.

"Mr. Taylor, were there two occasions in one week when your car was damaged?"

"Yes, sir."

"Who slit your tires and damaged the side panel?"

"Maddison, did, sir. Well, at least the second time for sure."

"How do you know it was Maddison?"

"There was a security camera in the school parking lot the first time, and then I put a surveillance camera on my car for insurance purposes."

"I have no further questions. Counselor Brown?"

Maddie squirmed and looked away. She couldn't bear to look at Jake. "Mr. Taylor, why did the relationship with Maddison end?"

Maddie sat on the edge of her seat, anticipating, yet dreading, the answer.

"I threw her a surprise birthday party," Jake began. "I saw how mean she was to those outside and even inside her circle. It reminded me of when I was bullied in sports, and I wanted no part of it, or her."

"No further questions," Mr. Brown said. Maddie was sure he knew he was digging her grave. Jake walked back to the pew without looking at Maddie at all. From the corner of her eye, she could see Chloe hug him as he sat next to her.

It was the sheriff's turn to have his say.

"Sheriff Kirby, can you tell us the trouble Miss Hunter has gotten into lately?"

"Oh, I certainly can." He was enjoying his moment in the spotlight. "This young lady instigated vandalism of the Harwoods' home and car. She continuously cyberbullied poor young Miss Harwood, verified electronically by our tech experts. She bullied Miss Harwood at school, at the park, at the ice-skating rink, and everywhere she had the opportunity."

Maddie felt quite odd like she was outside her body. Like they were all talking about someone else. Like she wasn't even here.

Mr. Brown declined to cross-examine the sheriff. Elmo was the next to take the oath.

"Please tell me about the phone you invented for the Kind Heart Club, Mr. Blaze," the DA asked.

"When I heard about the Kind Heart Club from Nancy Peterson, the new therapist at Pine Cove High, I had an idea to invent some phone operating software to focus on kindness." Elmo was speaking quietly, but you could hear a pin drop in the room. "It would be a phone that would only transmit kind messages. It is useless for unkind words or cyberbullying. It is also able to do much more. Such as letting the user know, through creative content and video, what could have been when the user has made a poor decision," Elmo explained. "And that's not all it can do ..."

"I think that is sufficient," the DA cut in. "I believe we get the gist of it all, most of us not being tech-savvy individuals. You did invent the phone, correct?"

"Yes, sir, with a couple of other people," Elmo answered.

"And Miss Hunter stole the phone from the counselor's office?"

"I believe so, sir."

"That is all I need."

Again, Peter Brown declined to cross-examine, which appeared to perturb Elmo. He shrugged his shoulders, obviously disappointed he would not be allowed to say more.

"That brings us to Miss Nancy Peterson," Judge Wilson determined.

Nancy seemed rather uncomfortable as she swore in and took her seat. Maddie guessed the court scene was bringing back bad memories for her.

The DA ripped into Nancy without wasting any time.

"Miss Peterson, you are a therapist at Pine Cove High School?"

"Yes, sir. I am."

"And you have been there for how many years?"

"I've been there for one ... month."

"Well, then you must still be in the honeymoon phase, out to turn everything around ... you know, overly ambitious."

Nancy paused, looked at Maddie, and answered. "That's a matter of perception. But, yes, I do feel I can be a great help."

The DA took a long moment to look Nancy up and down. "How many times, Miss Peterson, have you *done* time? You know ... how many times have you been to prison?"

There were gasps in the crowd.

Nancy composed herself. "Three, and that's why—"

"Mmm. No further questions, your Honor."

Nancy glanced back over to Maddie and shook her head.

"Counsel?" Judge Wilson asked Mr. Brown, giving him a chance to let Nancy speak. "I have no questions," Mr. Brown declared.

The judge looked at Mr. Brown, puzzled. "Really, Counselor? Then, I will do something a little unconventional here ... a wee bit out of the box, if you will. This case has turned the community upside down, without a doubt. The town, and Miss Harwood, deserve closure. I don't see that happening the way this court is unfolding. I am going to call Grace Harwood, herself, to the stand. She has asked to speak, and I fully believe she deserves the chance, minus the interrogation. Miss Harwood."

Maddie had not seen Grace in the crowd. She felt sick as Grace emerged in her Sunday school suit, very similar to her own. She looked thin and frail, much as she did on the mountain. "You may proceed when you are ready," the judge told her.

Grace began. "I would like to say that it is true; Maddie Hunter did bully me, in person, on the phone, on my laptop, in class, at school, at the park, at the Hut, and just about everywhere else. She has hated me for years. She was responsible for making me fall in love with someone who didn't exist, Hayden. I went with my entire family to meet him at The Birdhouse restaurant and suddenly realized the joke was on me."

Maddie felt one inch tall. She could feel all the eyes in the courtroom staring at her.

"I ran away from the restaurant and wanted to die. I'd had enough. It was too much. I was too ashamed to tell my parents the truth that Hayden was not a real person. I ran to the mountain and got lost. I finally found the cave and was too afraid to leave. I was cold and sick and weak.

Then Maddie came. She found me when no one else did. She saved me, and I know that deep down, Maddie has a kind heart. It was just all covered up."

Maddie looked at Grace and smiled. What she said probably wouldn't make a difference in the outcome of the court. But it meant the world to her.

"Thank you, Miss Harwood, for your touching testimony," Judge Wilson said. "You may go back to your seat now. You are a courageous girl."

Grace walked back to her place next to her parents and brother. "Now, I would like to hear from the defendant, Maddison Hunter."

Maddie was stunned. She never expected to be called to talk. Mr. Brown had told her she would not be allowed to speak. She was frozen in her seat, unable to move.

She looked at her attorney. He shrugged. "Better do what the man says," he advised.

Maddie looked out and spotted Grandma Betty, Ashley, and Liam. She drew a breath of courage. For them, she had to do her best.

"Miss Hunter, please tell us your version of the crime spree you've been on. Remember, you are sworn in. So, what you say should not be selective ... trying to get out of being found guilty, that is," the judge instructed.

Maddie began to go over her actions, not stopping to think about anything before she spoke. Let them all hear it straight from her mouth.

"Grace is right. I hated her, and I was mean. Like Echo told you, we had the Scarlet Squad group, and I was the leader. Anyone different, how they looked, acted or thought ... top target. I didn't think much about them or their feelings. It was all about mine. It made me feel good. When Grace went missing, I knew if she died, I killed her. That's too far. I am mean, but I'm not evil. I had to find her. And I did. I borrowed the ATV and took the phone I had stolen. Wrongs don't make rights, but I did find her. I would have done anything to find her. Then, I brought her back to her family." Maddie found Grace and her family in the ocean of faces. She continued, "because I had taken her from her family."

"Interesting," the judge said. "Do go on, Miss Hunter."

"Then ... I went to jail. I deserve to be here, but Nancy's right. It's scary. Nancy turned out to be right about a lot of stuff. I wish I had listened to her earlier."

The judge took a drink of water. "Miss Peterson, can you join us up here?"

Nancy was caught off guard. She walked up to the judge's desk, ran her finger through her hair, and stood waiting for further instructions.

"You said you went to prison, not just jail – but prison – three times?" he asked, wrinkling his eyebrows with concern.

"Yes, your Honor."

"What leads you to believe that you, of all people, can help Miss Hunter, who has been quite intent on stirring up trouble all over town for quite some time?"

"Well, because I didn't have anyone to mentor me. I was in it all alone, and I believe, I honestly believe, that there is a caring and kind heart to be salvaged here," Nancy said.

Judge Wilson slammed his gavel on the desk. "I hereby sever this case from being the State versus Maddison Hunter. I am going to bring an additional charge against Pine Cove High School. In the State of Colorado, schools can be held liable for incidents of violence such as bullying that occur at school. Colorado is not playing, and neither am I. Principal Freeman, please approach the bench," he demanded.

Mr. Freeman made his way down the aisle. He was sweating hard, and his glasses were sliding off his nose.

"What do you propose I do with this case? What do you and your constituents have to offer as a solution to this legal implication?" Judge Wilson asked in a harsh voice.

Mr. Freeman looked blank. "May I have a word with Miss Peterson?" he asked.

"You may," the judge agreed.

The principal turned to speak Nancy beside him. Then he turned back to the judge. "We have a plan," he said.

Judge Wilson raised his eyebrow. "And ..."

"We would like to petition that Miss Hunter be subject to being an active member of the Kind Heart Club. And that the only electronic device she is allowed to communicate through be the kindness phone."

The judge glanced over at Maddie, still in the witness chair. "Miss Hunter, will you approach the bench?"

Maddie was finding it difficult to breathe. Her heart was racing too fast and beating strongly. She was painfully aware of everyone in the crowd: her grandmother, sister, Grace, Echo, Jake, and Chloe. She slowly approached the judge.

This is where they send me away to prison and throw away the key. I know it is.

"Miss Hunter," Judge Wilson began. "In case you think I have forgotten, I know, personally, that your misbehavior began many years ago, by way of a criminal destruction of a treehouse." Maddie's eyes popped. She dared not utter a word.

"But I am also aware that you've not had a fair shot in life," he continued, rubbing his chin in deep thought. "Your mother, well, she is not fit to be your guardian in her current state. I can and will recommend your mother be sent to rehab, but the rest is up to her. Likewise, the decisions you make from here on out are up to you. It's a game called life."

Judge Wilson slammed his gavel down on his

desk. "I hereby sentence you, Maddison Hunter, to five years in a State of Colorado Juvenile Detention Center."

Maddie felt her world falling apart.

"Probated!" the judge added. "Deferred Adjudicated. Which means that if you fail to comply with certain conditions, you *will* do the five years."

Maddie was so relieved she thought she would pass out. "Thank you, your Honor," she whispered. "Thank you."

"Oh, I'm not through," the judge said. "You will be required to attend every meeting of the Kind Heart Club, and you will have no electronic communication outside of the kindness phone. We do have a slight problem, though. Your mother should be in rehab for at least three months. Now, where does that leave you? Your grandmother is too elderly to deal with you. She did her time when she raised your mother; God bless her soul. I can see your sister has her hands full with the baby. You, most assuredly, cannot be alone. Is there anyone in this court who would volunteer to foster this child through her probation period?"

A man stood from the audience and walked with a limp to the judge's desk. Although she hadn't seen him for ten years, Maddie recognized him immediately. Dad.

She had always imagined this moment. Dad would come back for her and apologize for leaving. Say how much he loved her. Say it was all mom's fault, that he'd never wanted to go. Maddie would run up and hug him and feel safe.

But she didn't feel safe. Seeing him made her gut churn strangely. "Announce yourself," the judge directed.

"Axel Hunter. Maddison's father," Dad said.

Oh, that voice. Maddie remembered that voice yelling.

There was a rustle in the room. The bailiff appeared and whispered something to the judge. "All right," he conceded. "Ladies and gentlemen," he began. "Elodie Hunter has requested to have a word with the court."

A hush fell on the crowd. Maddie's heart began to race all over again. *Why does she have to ruin everything?* She cringed at the thought of being embarrassed by her mother one more time.

Elodie approached the judge. "I know I am a bad and horrible mother," she began. "I drink too much, don't cook, and don't make much money either. But I love my daughters. I am not the one who left them as he did. But yes ... I *made* him leave. After he started beating me, I knew it was a matter of time before he'd abuse them too. So, I did everything in my power to make him leave, and ... he did."

She turned to Maddie. "I know you've always hated me for running your father off," she said with a slight choke. "But I did it for you ... and for your sister."

She looked at the judge. "I am begging you not to let him take her. There's no telling where his head's at after all these years. I'll do whatever it takes to clean up and be a better mother, but you can't let her go with him."

Maddie couldn't believe what she was hearing. She didn't want to believe it. It was easier to think that her dad left just because he couldn't stand her mother, not because he was abusive. "And you never told anyone?" the judge asked, bewildered.

Elodie lowered her head. "I was afraid to tell the authorities because we'd have ended up in court. I didn't tell the girls because I'd rather look like the bad person than for them to really know what a creep their father was ... or is. He has money ... and power. All I know is I did the best I could."

"Well, that certainly leaves this case in limbo," Judge Wilson said, scratching his head. "Mr. Hunter, you are dismissed from this court. Who else will watch over this child until if and when her mother gets her act together?"

Nancy immediately stood to her feet. "I will!" she exclaimed. "I will be happy to watch over her for however long it takes until she has a good, safe place to go."

Maddie was stunned. She hadn't even known Nancy for long, and she was willing to look after her?

"You may change some things in the school and with this young lady after all. You are off to a good start," Judge Wilson said. "All right. Maddison, you've got one chance. I suggest you make good use of it."

"I will," Maddie promised, finally catching her breath again.

The judge thought for a moment. "Oh, and no contact with Grace," he added. "I object!" a voice cried in the crowd.

There was total silence. Grace stood to her feet. "Your Honor, please. Maddie saved my life, and I believe we have some making up of lost time to do. I think we got a good start to a friendship while we were up on the mountain."

Judge Wilson was quiet for a good long time. Then, he stood up, slammed his hammer down, and stated, "So be it! The court is adjourned."

Maddie was free to leave. It all felt surreal. So much had happened, her head was spinning, and a million questions flooded her mind. Did her mother *really* love her? Was her father as bad as her mother said, or was he now a changed man? Why had so many people spoken up for her? Had they liked her all along? How had she spun so far out of control?

She was suddenly overwhelmed with emotions. She felt awkward, embarrassed, and vulnerable. Like she had been standing before the court naked. And in a way, she had been. Stripped of her defenses, now she had to face the world without hiding behind bullying. It was terrifying.

Nancy walked over to her and whispered, "Everything's going to work out, Mad." She drew Maddie's attention to her butterfly tattoo. "We'll wing it ... together."

Maybe she's right. She has been right about everything else so far.

Nancy took her arm, and together they walked out of the courtroom. When they stepped out the door, the blinding sunlight caught Maddie off-guard and took her breath.

"Are you alright?" Nancy asked.

Maddie nodded. "I guess I just didn't realize how dark it was in there."

Nancy smiled. "Yes, sometimes it's hard to notice the darkness until you're in the light."

"That makes sense ... in a weird kind of way."

As Grace walked past with her family, she stopped for a moment and asked. "Are you alright?"

"I'm OK," Maddie said with a reassuring smile. "How 'bout you?"

Grace managed a smile but didn't answer. She seemed nervous. Was she still afraid of her? If so, she couldn't blame her. She knew her actions had caused a lot of pain to Grace, and she expected it would take a while for her to heal. Maddie knew that in saving Grace, it was Grace who had saved her, and she was and always would be eternally grateful to her. It might take a lifetime to prove that, but it was a new day, and a new year was right around the corner. As long as Grace was alive, there was hope. And... she was.

ACKNOWLEDGMENTS

Thank you to everyone who has contributed ideas, professional assistance, and support. Without them, this book and the other swirling around in my mind could not have burst into life. They have enabled the creation of this book by filling the void of what I did not know and could not do. The following people have made a dream come true, and I am genuinely grateful to them.

Cheryl Jerabek, whose love of the written word knows no bounds.

My editor Jessica Hoadley kept me in check and crafted "If Grace is Dead I Killed Her" into a substantially better book than in its infancy.

Lorna Reid and Carmen Mudie for valuable help in the preparation of the manuscript.

Brett Mudie and Kirstie Minifie generously gave up their time and knowledge, patiently listening to my ideas and proposing better ones. Their limitless creativity and passion for marketing have proved invaluable. Kirstie took a simple concept for a book cover and created a masterpiece.

Emma and Keeley Robinson, Emma, Ella, and Libby Stawicki, Ceri, Tiffany, Charlie Warwicker, and Delainie Howard provided great insights into the lives and minds of teenage girls.

David Beard a wise and thoughtful supporter and wordsmith.

Dr. Toby Miles-Johnson's brilliant idea changed the course of this book.

My family and friends always supported me and gave me the space to create the first book in Golden Series, even though I have missed the occasional social event and the odd glass of wine.